# Tales
## from a
# Sick Bed

Also by L.P. Howarth published by Catnip

**Bodyswap: The Boy who was 84**
**Tales from a Sick Bed: Brainstorms**
**Tales from a Sick Bed: Fever Dreams**

# Tales from a Sick Bed

## The Medicine Chest

# L. P. HOWARTH

Catnip

CATNIP BOOKS
Published by Catnip Publishing Ltd
14 Greville Street
London EC1N 8SB

This edition first published 2009
1 3 5 7 9 10 8 6 4 2

A CIP catalogue record for this book is available from the British Library.

ISBN 978 1 846470 84 4

Printed in Poland

www.catnippublishing.co.uk

# Contents

A Bug's Going Round    7

UFO    10

The Comfi-Lux    37

Bigglesmith    62

NICK    90

# A Bug's Going Round

You know when you're ill in bed, and everything looks larger than life, kind of super-real and out-of-scale, as though something as big as a gorilla in the wardrobe is about to reveal itself?

You're hot – very hot. Your stomach and neck are like a furnace. A bug going around, Mum says.

Maybe it got stuck in your throat.

The chocolate bar beside your bed tastes metallic and weird. Even its wrapper looks like something you never saw before in your life. When you open your eyes again, it's gone. In its place is a bowl of cold soup. You never recognized it to start with, and it tasted of cosmic doormats sprinkled with spacedust.

'Mum!' you call weakly, 'where's that chocolate?'

'What . . . chocolate?'

And you see your strange face in the mirror, and wonder: An Unidentified Food Item — was it ever there at all?

Hours later you sink deeply into the duvet and the bed enfolds you and protects you from school, from real life. You may never have to get up at all, if you only surrender to it . . .

The bed came in humungous pieces, like something from Cinderella's stage-set. You thought it was ugly, monstrous. Now you luxuriate in its individually-pocketed springs, while the Comfi-Lux takes over your mind. Ill in bed for three days, now? You won't be getting better anytime soon . . .

Bigglesmith! Suddenly you sit up in bed.

Did you dream it? What a word — a word, sounding silly, which everyone agrees to agree, makes everything STOP AT ONCE.

Even being ill all day.

A word to stop brothers and sisters bugging you. A word to stop mates ringing you up and hassling you to come back to school tomorrow. A word to stop all unfairness, ever. A word to end all World Wars.

Bigglesmith, enough with being ill! Bigglesmith, stop with the chicken soup! Bigglesmith, with being in bed!

Bigglesmith, get out, and get on with your life! Bigglesmith! Bigglesmith! Bigglesmith!

So then, the next evening you're watching her smoking? 'Mum, don't.'

She stubs it out. 'It's my last.'

You know it isn't. 'How d'you expect me to stay well, if I'm passive smoking?'

'I told you, I've given it up.'

'Yeah, right.'

You've almost given up trying to make her. That's until you meet Nick . . .

# UFO

'So,' Mr Hatt said, 'what do you think?'

We all groaned – wouldn't you? Design and market a chocolate bar. Some CDT project, right?

'First, think out your approach,' Hatters droned. 'Will the product be fruit or nut-based? What will your chocolate bar's *image* be? Will it be a biscuit bar for the mid-morning snack market, or is it definitely a luxury product? What about texture? Will it be crunchy or creamy? Dark chocolate or light? What about packaging? If you're clear about product profile from the word go, you'll be streets ahead when it comes to design and graphics –'

'Can it be like a Yorkie?' Maxwell Harris asked. 'Sir, can it be like a Yorkie?'

'– so I'm saying think-it-through-from-the-start. Are you with me, Gavin Blatchford?'

'Sir,' Gavin said.

'What am I saying?'

'Um, think about texture.'

'And?'

'It's important to think it through.'

'Yeah, right,' Claire Sales said, '*really* important. What are we, curing cancer?'

'You might not think, Claire Sales, that marketing matters,' Hatters said, in his serious voice, 'but you wouldn't be wearing those shoes or carrying that bag, if it didn't. The lesson economics gives us here, is that . . .'

Mr Hatt droned on about marketing products on the world stage and the importance of a well-designed item, etc., etc. So much for Craft, Design and Technology *that* day. At the end of the lesson he said, 'Right, 9H, Assignment Sheets. I'd advise you to read them through carefully and take it a step at a time.'

Good thing I don't have much work on, I thought. Good thing it won't take ages to do. I couldn't believe it when I saw it:

*CDT Spring Term Design Project, 9H*
*Design and market a chocolate bar, with particular reference to advertising, product profile and cost analysis. Considering your target consumer group and*

*the likely appeal of any packaging, produce a complete advertising campaign to include product research, initial design, prototype packaging, advertising images/slogans, posters, etc. Assessments will take into account individual initiative and public relations/press schemes for launching your product. Completion date – to be given.*

'This'll take *ages*,' Max Harris moaned. 'Do we *have* to, sir?'

'Not if it's too much trouble,' Mr Hatt said, seriously. 'Take the rest of your life off instead,'

'How will you manage in a design crisis,' Claire asked Max sarcastically, 'if you don't design something pointless in school and think it through from the start?'

'That'll do, I think, Claire,' Mr H. told Claire Sales. 'Cynicism can be useful, up to a point.'

'What point is that, Mr Hatt?'

'The point, Claire, at which it becomes tiresome and counter-productive. What will *your* product be – acid drops, I wonder?'

'It has to be a chocolate bar, doesn't it? That's what the Assignment Sheet says.'

'I'm joking, of course.'

'Of course.'

You don't often see Hatters rattled. Claire Sales was on top form that day. But it was pointless arguing. We'd have to do the project anyway, no matter *how* boring it sounded. The funny thing was, though, it wasn't too boring at all. Everyone had an opinion about chocolate bars, even, and including, the olds. Soon as I got home I asked Mum, '"*Design and market a chocolate bar, with particular reference to advertising, product profile and cost analysis.*" So what do you think?' I asked.

'What do I think about what?'

'*Design and market a chocolate bar, with parti—*'

'Yes, I got that. So what?'

'So how would *you* do it, d'you think?'

Mum thought. 'First, I'd think up a name.'

'Mr Hatt says think up a filling.'

'That just shows how wrong he can be. Take it from me,' Mum said, 'it's all in the name.'

Mum was right. I started noticing chocolate-bars, after that. I mean, I noticed them *all*, not just the ones I buy. As well as the usual names, I noticed Twistas, Spree, Whorl, Snap and Nutz that I hadn't noticed before. I made a note of them. It's called market research. That's what I told Mr Tandy in Le Bon Bon. Le Bon Bon's not French, or anything. It's only the best sweet shop in the High Street, where everyone goes after school. Mr Tandy's got big thick eyebrows. Everyone notices them. Soon as I told him about my research, he raised them straightaway.

'I have to look at chocolate bars,' I asked.

'You *have* to? That's a new one.'

'Market research,' I told Mr Tandy. Mr Tandy knows me by sight. I'm always in Le Bon Bon for pick'n'mix. 'Market research,' I told him, 'for my project.'

'I've heard a lot of excuses in my time but that one takes the biscuit.' Mr Tandy said.

Le Bon Bon's a cool sweet shop. Mr Tandy knows what he's doing. As well as every kind of chocolate bar, he keeps quality selections for the old dears plus stuff like prawns, brains, shrimps, jellies and cola bottles for people – like me – who're into stuff like that.

'Can I have a quarter of jelly babies?' I said.

'Is this market research, as well?'

'They're just to eat while I'm thinking.'

'Of course,' said Mr Tandy. 'Just to help you think.'

I got out my research file. 'So how many Twistas do you sell? Are Twistas a popular line?' A popular line. It sounded good. I'd picked that up in class.

'I don't know about a popular line,' Mr Tandy said, 'but they go quite well when school turns out on a weekday.'

I made a note in my research file. *Twista*, I wrote. *Sells quite well on weekdays.*

'How about Whorls?'

'The same.'

'And Caramix?'

'Only the toffee flavour. Kids don't like caramel and coffee.'

'And what about image?' I said. 'What kind of people go for Cruisers, would you say?'

'People like me,' said Mr Tandy. 'I like a Cruiser, myself.'

*Cruisers. People like Mr Tandy*, I wrote. Probably there was a direct marketing link between people with thick eyebrows and chocolate-coated peanut Cruisers (Take Your Time With A Cruiser). It only wanted a bit of research to join the dots. So many chocolate bars, so little time. I'd had no idea it was such a hot subject. It had sounded so *nothing* to begin with.

'Brilliant,' I said. 'You've been a big help. Thanks a lot, Mr Tandy.'

Next CDT lesson, when Mr Hatt asked me to name my Top Three Marketing Priorities, which he did about twenty minutes into the lesson, I brought out my file and said, 'Name. Image. Filling. In that order.'

'Right,' Mr H. said. 'Good thinking. Now we're getting somewhere. Who's done some market research?'

'Me, Mr Hatt.' Gavin Blatchford put up his fat hand. 'I bought sweets before school *three days* this week. I got the wrappers, see?' He brought out a load of them, the pig – Whizzas, Meltdowns, Milkos, Zen Bars, Smoothies, Toppas, Treat, Flamenco, Sin City, Slyders, Double Choc Dark Brazil Twist, the works. Unbelievable. Every chocolate bar you could think of.

'Good – good work.' Hatters didn't know what to say. 'Not *exactly* what I had in mind, Gavin.'

That's what I *call* market research.' Gavin burped. He looked around, stupid fat toad that he is. 'I just about ate every chocolate bar up the supermarket.'

'Yes,' said Mr H., 'yes, I can see you have. Anyone got any detailed design ideas?'

No one said anything.

'Rita, how about you?'

'Um, I thought about a chocolate bar called OTT – for Over The Top,' Rita Neale said, so quietly you could hardly hear her. Mr Hatt always asks her. He thinks she's good, or something. 'Or I thought about one called The Works.'

'The Works is good,' Max Harris said. 'That's a good name, The Works.'

'Yeah, right,' said Claire Sales. 'I can imagine going into a shop and asking for The Works.'

'Or an OTT,' I said. 'An OTT's all right.'

'It's all right,' Claire said, 'it's not brilliant.'

'What did you think of, then?'

Claire made a face. 'I thought about just, you know, chocolate and stuff. What kind of chocolate people like.'

'You haven't thought of anything, have you?'

'An anxious world waits,' Claire said.

'Don't strain yourself,' Max Harris told her. 'We wouldn't want you bursting a blood-vessel or anything.'

'Not much chance of that,' Claire said. 'What's your idea? Double Choc No Brain? Waste-of-Space wrapped in lush milk chocolate and hazelnuts?'

'Funny,' said Max, 'ha, ha. You should be on telly.'

'I am,' Claire said. 'It's just that you haven't noticed.'

'To-return-to-your-Design-Brief, 9H.' Mr Hatt stood up and rapped his desk. 'I'd like your initial design sketches in by this time next week – is that the bell? What does that *mean*, Gavin Blatchford?'

'End of the lesson, sir.'

'Very funny. I'll ask you again what that *means*.'

'Design sketches in by this time next week,' Gavin mumbled.

'Without fail,' Mr Hatt said.

Almost exactly a week later, 'How about Marx Bars?' Mum said, over the Sunday-evening ironing. 'What do you think? It came to me last night.'

'What did?' I asked her. Not that I cared.

I'd gone all listless and floppy about it, in any case. I was on the point of giving up over CDT and handing in *any* old idea. I was too tired. It was too late. I didn't care, anyway.

'Marx Bars.' Mum said, again.

'You keep saying Marx Bars, what do you *mean*?'

I was getting pretty irritated by this time. It wasn't Mum's fault it had actually got to the *last night* before handing in initial design ideas for CDT. The reason I felt irritated was, I didn't exactly have any. The design cupboard was bare. Any initial ideas had stayed that way. For another reason, I'd done a *major* geography project over the last week and I wasn't about to lose any sleep over Hatter's chocolate-bar scam. That's what I told myself, anyway.

'After the Marx Brothers – you know,' Mum said, 'Groucho, Chico, Harpo and – Zeppo, I think. They made funny films called *Duck Soup* and *Monkey Business*, and Groucho had a big thick moustache and a funny walk. You could have Marx *Bars* with a brand-name *identity*, then have a different filling for each bar, like a Groucho could be dark chocolate with ginger – a bit of a bite – and, I don't know, a Chico could be peanuts –'

'No, Mum,' I said.

'Why not?'

'It's old-fashioned, for one thing. No one would know what it means.'

'No one under thirty perhaps.'

'That's what I mean,' I said.

*Clump, clump, clump* – Mum clumped the iron around on Dad's shirt-front as though clubbing the old ironing-board to death would somehow end ironing for ever.

'Like a cup of tea?' she asked, after a moment.

'I'll make it,' I said, and put the kettle on. Then I said, 'I wouldn't mind getting a decent mark for CDT – just for *once*, I mean. I mean, I'm not that bothered. But I wouldn't mind, you know?'

# UFO

'You'll get there,' Mum said, 'I know you will. It just takes the right idea,'

*It just takes the right idea.* When I was lying in bed that night, it suddenly came to me. I'd been awake for ages thinking up names for chocolate bars, when I got so I couldn't stop. No *way* could I go to sleep, I'd stayed awake thinking so long. It had seemed amazingly hard to think up names for chocolate bars when I'd tried to think of them in class. Suddenly it seemed so easy. Blitz, Nirvana, Rappa Bar, Lush, Heaven, Choc-U-Like, Luvverly, Droolz, Gorge. I couldn't stop. Every time I tried to turn over and go to sleep a million ideas came crowding in, and they seemed pretty good to me, the way ideas you get in the middle of the night always look good until you think about them next morning. Then suddenly I got this brainstorm. It just popped into my mind. That was the way it happened.

The Unfeasibly Fabulous Object – UFO for short – *ultimate chocolate-bar heaven.* It was brilliant.

Why hadn't I thought of it before? A name that tripped off your tongue, without tying you down to any particular filling. They could have *different* fillings every so often. Why not? That could be a marketing point. Mr H. was keen on marketing points. Plus the ad campaign would be so *easy.* I could see the slogan now: UFO – Out Of This World – the Ultimate Chocolate Experience.

I could see it all so clearly. It wouldn't let me go. I tossed and turned for what seemed like hours, and *still* it came back and *would* make me think it out. Eventually I got out of bed and went downstairs. I tried boring myself to sleep with Dad's paper, but no matter what I read, I couldn't get the Unfeasibly Fabulous Object out of my mind. Every article in the *Evening Herald* that night seemed like it'd been *deliberately designed* to remind me; 'MIND OVER MATTER IN CROP CIRCLE PHENOMENON', 'RECORD CAR SALES OUT OF THIS WORLD', 'CHOCOLATE PHOBIA DROVE WOMAN WILD'. Even 'CAT IN ROCKET SHOCKER' set me thinking. They even had Readers' Weird Ones too:

*Send in Your Weirdest Story and Win Two Tickets to Rumblelow's Unknown Planets – Best Themed Ride in the West!*

Chocolate, rockets, out-of-this-world car sales. Your Weird Stories Featured – could there *be* anything more to remind me? In the end I designed the whole UFO campaign in the middle of the kitchen table at two o'clock in the morning. When I finally went back to bed the whole, thing was profiled, imaged, marketed and cost-assessed. Done. That simple. Or not.

Next morning I got up and thought about it. It still looked good to me. I told Dad, on his way out to work, and it looked good to Dad, as well.

'I had a brainstorm last night,' I said. 'UFO – what do you think?'

# UFO

'What d'you mean –' Dad said, loading his laptop into the car '– have you seen one?'

'I haven't *seen* one. I've *done* one. For CDT.'

'Tell me about it tonight. I haven't time for this now.'

'Yes, you have,' I said. 'All I want to know is, if you saw a chocolate bar called UFO, would you buy one?'

'Depends what was in it,' Dad said.

'But would you take a chance, even if you *didn't* know what was in it? If the wrapper looked good, I mean?'

'Once, maybe,' Dad said. 'I'm sorry. I've got to go.'

I got out my research file over breakfast and wrote, '*Middle-aged male market, impulse buy, once only*,' under UFO – Close Encounters of the Chocolate Kind. Then I packed away my file and ate two bowls of Weetos, straight off. I felt I deserved it, you know? But things were as different, that morning, as if the air'd gone blue or the trees had gone bendy or frogs had dropped out of the sky. It took me a while to realize.

The whole thing stopped being funny, as if it ever was, and started being seriously weird that morning, the morning after I dreamed up – just in time – the Unfeasibly Fabulous Object. I got out my file on the bus to school. I was really pleased with my design, a dark blue wrapper with UFO in glowing green letters. I'd used my fluorescent marker pen. It looked really good in the dark. If you fancied a UFO bar in the cinema, you'd be able to see to unwrap it; plus, it looked really cool. Mr Hatt, I thought, would be proud of me. I'd thought it through from the start. All the design sketches had the same graphics, like the wrapper, the posters and slogans. It was a really co-ordinated approach, plus I'd thought out some killer marketing points – really professional, I thought. But I wanted some feedback badly. Mum and Dad were no good. They wouldn't know cool if it bit them.

Soon as I got to school I showed Claire Sales my design file. I was pretty safe, showing Claire Sales. Too cool to copy anyone else's work, she was far too lazy, as well.

'UFO.'

'That's right,' I said.

Claire looked at my prototype wrapper.

'The Unfeasibly Fabulous Object,' I explained. 'It's chocolate-coated with three different fillings – you never know which one you'll get. Out Of This World – Beyond Chocolate to Infinity – that's the slogan.'

'How did you think of *that*?' Claire said.

'Why,' I said, 'don't you like it?'

'It's too *good*,' Claire complained. 'What's the matter with you? Hatters'll make me do mine again. Can't you hand in something rubbish?'

It *was* too good. Claire Sales was right. Mr Hatt went mad over my design folder. He practically *ate* my prototype wrapper, he drooled over it so much. Plus he *actually held up my rough sketches* and waved them in front of the class. 'These are what I *call* initial designs,' Hatters raved. 'This kind of work just shows what can be done with a little imagination – Maxwell Harris, are we taking this in?'

*So* embarrassing. Now everyone would hate me, of course. It's started already, I thought, when no one hardly spoke to me at lunchtime. I couldn't help counting the Twix in the vending machine. It's a funny thing. Once you start noticing chocolate bars, it's hard to make yourself stop.

That night, the sightings began. It all started with Dad.

'You know those UFOs,' Dad said over tea, 'I saw one on my way home –'

'You saw a UFO?'

'– and I meant to get one, but I bumped into Oliver Kitchen – he's looking a lot older these days, his wife's a receptionist at Priory Mount, now –'

'Dad,' I said, 'what are you talking about?'

'These new chocolate bars,' Dad said. 'Aren't they what you were talking about this morning?'

'What new chocolate bars?'

'UFOs. I told you, I meant to get one.'

My whole life flashed before my eyes, I don't mind telling you.

'*You mean, you saw a chocolate bar called a UFO?*'

'Are you having trouble with your hearing? I stopped to get some petrol and I noticed they had those UFOs you were talking about, when I bumped into Oliver –'

23

'What are they like?'

'I-don't-know-I-didn't-get-one. Poor Olly Kitchen,' Dad said. 'He's almost unrecognizable, he's aged so much since I last –'

'What do they *look* like, I mean?'

'I don't know. Blue and green wrapper –'

'Like *this*?' I opened my file. All my designs spilled out. My sketches, posters, prototype wrapper – in shades of blue and green.

'That's it,' Dad said, 'very nice. Why did you have to draw it?'

'I didn't draw it, I *designed* it. I told you I did, this morning.'

'But you didn't, did you?' Dad said. 'I mean to say, they're real.'

'No, Dad, I made them up. Last night, in fact – ask Mum. We have to design a chocolate bar, and UFO's my idea. We had CDT fourth lesson. Mr Hatt really likes my designs.'

'Have it your way,' Dad said. 'Perhaps you copied it subconsciously.'

'I couldn't have copied *anything*. You must have made a mistake when you were talking to Oliver Kitchen. I made up UFOs they *don't exist*, all right?'

'I'll get one tomorrow,' Dad said. 'Then you'll see I'm right.'

'I won't, because you're not.'

'I am.'

'You're not.'

'I am.'

'Dad.'

'I know what I saw'

'Bet you three quid you didn't.'

'Bet you five I did.'

I shook my head. You *sad* man. But, still, it made me think.

Next morning: 'Mum,' I said, 'what's copyright?'

'Copyright.' Mum thought. 'It means something *belongs* to you. Only *you* have the *right* to *copy* it. No one else can take your idea. Like *James and the Giant Peach* is Copyright Roald Dahl.'

'That's what I thought,' I said. 'Dad says I copied my chocolate bar.'

'I wouldn't worry about him,' Mum said. 'He's probably got it all wrong. He can't remember the name of something I've asked him to get at the shops for more than two minutes.'

'But what if somebody steals my idea?'

'I wouldn't show it to Claire Sales,' Mum said. 'That Claire Sales'd think nothing of copying your work.'

'I mean, suppose you invented something, then someone said you hadn't – or someone invented the *same thing –*'

'Oh,' Mum said, 'I see.'

'I mean, how could you prove you thought of it?'

'Well, there's the patents office. Or you could post it to yourself.'

'Post it to *yourself*?'

'That's right,' Mum said. 'You write down your idea, whatever it is, then you post it to yourself in a sealed envelope, then the postmark proves the date you thought of it.'

'*Brilliant*,' I said. And it was. I went straight up the post office after school. Stuck three of my rough sketches plus a photocopy of my wrapper design in an envelope. Posted it to myself. Simple. Copyright Crabbe Creations, 1997. The post office is next to Le Bon Bon. I thought I'd just slip in.

'Hi, Mr Tandy,' I said.

'Still doing market research?'

'Yes,' I said, 'I am. Got any UFOs?'

Mr Tandy's eyebrows shot up. 'Are you trying to be funny?'

'No I said, 'it's a chocolate bar –'

'I've never seen one *in my ljfe*.' His face had gone really white. 'Who's been telling tales?'

'Mr Tandy,' I said, 'I don't know –'

'I hope it's not starting again.'

'What?' I said. 'Mr Tandy, what's not starting again?'

'The old trouble – UFOs.' Mr Tandy brought out his

handkerchief and mopped his forehead. He had kind of a Welsh accent. I hadn't noticed before. 'Bringing it right to my face. I thought we'd left all that behind us, when we came here and opened Le Bon Bon.'

'All what, Mr Tandy?' I said. 'I don't know what you mean.'

'Between you and me,' Mr Tandy said, '*never you go admitting it, if you ever see anything strange.* I did, and it ruined my life, *and* my wife Beryl's, as well. It got in all the papers. We had to move house in the end.'

'Why? What happened?' I said. Mr Tandy seemed pretty upset.

'We left the area completely. We had to, see, in the end. You see, I saw a UFO – an Unidentified Flying Object, a space-ship, whatever you want to call it. I saw a UFO once, and *they never let me forget it.*'

'Where did you live before?' I said. I wished I'd never come in.

'Pontypridd,' Mr Tandy said. 'That's where I saw it, see? No one believed me at first. Then everyone thought I was mad. "Seen any funny lights lately?" they said. "Seen any little green men?"'

'I'm sorry,' I said, 'I didn't know. I didn't mean anything.'

'Business dropped off after that, so we moved here and opened Le Bon Bon. It really was a nightmare, I can tell you.'

'People say things they don't mean,' I said, 'it doesn't mean anything –'

'It doesn't matter now.' Mr Tandy put away his handkerchief. 'As long as it doesn't start again. I have to think of Beryl, you see. Now then, what can I do for you?'

'It's just,' I said – I *had* to go on, now I'd started – 'it's just, my dad saw this chocolate bar – *thinks* he saw this chocolate bar – it's supposed to be new out, and it's called the Unfeasibly Fabulous Object, and the wrapper's blue and green, and I wondered if you'd seen it?'

'New one on me,' said Mr Tandy, 'and believe you me, I'd *know*.'

He would, too. I could've kissed him, eyebrows and all. My designs were safe. It *had* to be a mistake. *No one* could launch a new chocolate bar without Mr Tandy knowing about it and stocking it right away. 'Mr Tandy,' I said, 'if you hadn't moved house, you'd never have opened Le Bon Bon. I'm *glad* you moved.'

'Thanks for that,' Mr Tandy said. 'Help yourself to an Ice Pole.'

'Cheers, Mr Tandy,' I said. 'I hope I keep a sweet shop when I grow up.'

'Let me know when you do,' Mr Tandy had cheered up already. 'Cheeky monkey,' he said.

What a rollercoaster ride. What a day. At least Mr Tandy had told me what I needed to know. I felt pretty pleased with myself all the way home. It lasted all of ten minutes. Until I bumped into Maxwell Harris.

'All right?' Max said.

'All right.'

'I told my mum about your stuff last night.'

'My stuff?'

'In CDT. And my mum says you'll catch it when old Hatters sees 'em.'

'Sees what?' I asked wearily.

'Only UFO bars up the newsagent, as if you didn't know "Look, Mr Hatt,"' Max Harris put on a stupid voice, '"I designed a Wispa and a Crunchie. Aren't I clever?" You can't copy something *real*. What did you think? He wouldn't *notice*?'

Another sighting – or was it? I was starting to feel, well – cross.

'Look,' I said, 'have you *had* a UFO?'

'N-oo,' Max Harris admitted, 'n-oo, I haven't, but Mum has.'

'Did she *say* she had?'

'She *saw* one and next time she's *getting* one, and next time I'm bringing one *in*. Then you can do all your project again because you think you're so *clever*.'

'Thanks, Max,' I said, 'thanks a million.'

To make the end of a perfect day, I saw a bus round the corner. The eighty-nine to Cheap's Place and Chetley Range, to be exact. I kind of noticed the Awayday ad on the side of the bus as I crossed the road. *Let the Train Take the Strain*. Let *something* take it, I thought. Then I looked back at the bus.

It had to be a bad joke. The back end of the number eighty-nine to Cheap's Place and Chetley Range only said:

*Beyond Chocolate. Beyond Words. Beyond the Known Snack Universe. New from Haynes – UFO. CLOSE ENCOUNTERS OF THE CHOCOLATE KIND.*

Underneath was this giant picture. The designs in my CDT file had spilled out and covered a bus. *My* blue-and-green wrapper. *My* glowing-green writing. *My* idea. *My* slogan – *my* everything that I'd thought up in bed, and over the kitchen table at two o'clock in the morning – there, like the back end of a bus – *on* the back end of a bus – out of my head and into reality, when I hadn't even *told* anyone except my CDT group and Hatters. This is it, I thought. I've lost the plot *big* time on this one. I really thought I was going mad. I got home and thought, OK. One way or the other, Dad can prove it.

'Well?' I asked him, over tea. 'Did you get one, then?'

'One what?' Dad said, blank as usual.

'A UFO bar, of course. We had a bet on, remember?'

'Oh,' Dad said, '*that*. The funny thing is, I couldn't find one in my usual shop.'

'You couldn't?' I felt – all right. 'Did you go anywhere else?'

# UFO

'Well,' Dad said, 'I asked everywhere. The filling station didn't have them any more. They said – I don't know – they said they hadn't even had them to *begin* with. I even stopped off at Tandy's. If anyone's heard of them *he* will, I thought.'

'Mr Tandy hasn't got them,' I said, quickly. 'You didn't go in and ask him for a UFO, did you?'

'I did, as a matter of fact. He told me he didn't stock them. He gave me a funny look.'

'So you haven't actually *had* one?'

'Funny-looking eyebrows he's got, that man, I wonder sometimes if he –'

'Dad.'

'All right, all right, you win. I'm beginning to think I dreamed it.'

'I think you saw *something*, all right. Maybe some other chocolate bar.'

'Well,' Dad said, 'it's a mystery.'

'A mystery worth five pounds, I think.'

I'd won, but it didn't end there. *That bus*, I thought, I couldn't stop. *I didn't see that bus.* I just about had myself convinced that UFOs were *my idea* – had been all along – and that for some bizarre reason people kept thinking they saw them, when the number eighty-nine with its CLOSE ENCOUNTERS OF THE CHOCOLATE KIND poster kept driving into my mind and running down everything I thought I'd got sorted at last. But if

31

Dad was wrong, I could be, too. Supposing *I thought* I'd seen the poster on the bus, because that's what I'd been spacing on all day, but really I saw something else? Or maybe I really *had* subconsciously copied something I'd seen without knowing it. I was sure I hadn't. But it couldn't work both ways. Either I was mad or I wasn't. Either they were real – and no one I knew had actually *had* a UFO – or they weren't. In the end I couldn't stand it. I had to get it off my chest. Mum and Dad were useless. Next day I rang the paper.

'I've got a Weird One for you,' I said. 'Something for Readers' Stories.'

At least I'd publicize UFO, even if I *was* going mad. Hadn't Hatters *said* we'd get Brownie points for initiative and publicity? *Assessments will take into account individual initiative and public relations press schemes for launching your project.* Plus at least it would go on record, no less, that no matter what parallel universe we were in, *I know I thought of it first.*

That's what I said when I rang them. 'I thought you should know, I thought of it first,' I said. 'There's something going on,' I said. 'I want to speak to a reporter.'

One thing the UFO business taught me was that You Never Know. I might even win two tickets to Rumbelow's Unknown Planets, Best Themed Ride in the West. Weirder things have happened. That's what Anita said.

The reporter's name was Anita. I told her everything. We had a long talk and a laugh. She had a good sense of humour. She even gave me some tips on how to get into journalism. If I'd known it would be *that* easy, I'd've said something *way* before. 'It makes a good story' she said, 'You're right,' she said, 'it's weird. Let me get some background and ring you back.'

Anita made a couple of calls, one to a chocolate manufacturer. They asked me to drop in a few things. A photo, one or two drawings. Then I sat back and enjoyed myself. I knew now I wasn't mad. Finally the paper came out, and everyone else knew it, too. Everyone read the article. Mr Hatt even cut it out. He thinks a lot of the school, and the school got a mention, of course. But I think he was, well, proud of *me*. I've never known Hatters so chuffed.

'A commendation,' he announced last CDT lesson, 'for Design, Anticipation of Market Trends and Initiative in Publicizing a Product, for excellent work all round and *top marks* for the spring term Design Project.' He shook my hand. His eyes were glowing. 'Well *done*, Alex,' he said.

Then he read out the article. The *Evening Herald* had done me proud. Under a picture of me pulling my designs out of the envelope I'd posted them to myself in — remember? — to prove they were Copyright Mc, the article began:

## BOUNDARY LANE STUDENT IN 'PSYCHIC' CHOC BAR PUZZLER

'Sightings of a new milk-chocolate phenomenon have had an unexpected effect on a third-year student at Boundary Lane Community College. Alex Crabbe thought she'd seen Haynes' new UFO bar before it was launched – in her Craft, Design and Technology file at school – and she can prove it!

Dubbed the ultimate chocolate experience, Haynes Confectionery had planned the slow release of their new UFO bar at selected shops and supermarkets to test reaction to the new product before the official release date – but not before Alex, thirteen, had dreamed up her own UFO.

"I thought I was going mad," Alex said. "We had to design a chocolate bar for a school project, and at first I couldn't think of anything. Then the idea just popped into my head. I stayed up late and drew the designs on Sunday the eighth of March. A day or two later, the sightings began – all my friends said they'd seen a chocolate bar just like the one I designed! I never saw a UFO in my life until Haynes sent me a box of them yesterday – I think I must be psychic!"

The postage date on her detailed designs backs up Alex's story "I posted them to myself," she said. "I wanted to know how to copyright my idea. Mum says it's just as well I did!"

# UFO

A spokesman for Haynes Confectionery said, "This is a remarkable coincidence. Records show that Alex was extremely unlikely to have been exposed to UFO before the night she drew her detailed designs, identical with our original artwork. She had the whole concept to a T. It's incredible to think that Alex may have read our minds. There may be a future for Alex with Haynes – in predicting market developments!"

Now Alex has been awarded full marks at school – for a Design and Technology project so good, it turned out to be real!'

I got a letter from Haynes Confectionery the day after that. Their public relations department sent me a framed photocopy of the article, and a personal invitation to visit the factory from P. H. Stanley, Regional Director, Haynes Chocolate. I showed it to Mr Tandy.

'Well,' said Mr Tandy, 'we're coming up in the world.'

'Soon I'll be as famous as you,' I said.

'Me?' said Mr Tandy. 'I'm big in Pontypridd.'

'I didn't mean that,' I said.

'I know,' said Mr Tandy. 'See that you keep your feet on the ground. Then you can't go wrong,' he said.

I always keep my feet on the ground these days. *Never go admitting it, if you ever see anything strange.* At least I kept Mr Tandy's rule about *one* thing. I never *did* tell Dad I'd seen the poster on the back of the number eighty-nine to Cheap's Place and Chetley Range, when it might have proved he was right all along, when I might've owed *him* five quid. And do you know? I *never saw that bus again*, so I might've half-dreamed it, after all.

And yesterday I finally got to eat one. I undid the wrapper – my wrapper. I sank my teeth in (Three Different Fillings – Which Will You Encounter?) and, I have to say, UFO is a pretty cool chocolate bar. Better than anything *I* could dream up. *Beyond chocolate. Beyond words. Beyond the known snack universe.* It was lovely. Out of this World.

# The Comfi-Lux

*Over 1200 individual pocket springs in a 150cm (5ft)*
*mattress. Sumptuous layers of fillings give a truly luxurious*
*sleeping experience*, said the label on the mattress.

*Sumptuous layers of fillings. A truly luxurious experience.*
It sounded like a cake. But it wasn't a cake, it was a bed.
A giant of a bed. A monster. Her parents' new bed – the
Comfi-Lux King Size, to be exact. Lola looked it over
with distaste. Its pompous stripped-pine headboard
complete with knobs and flourishes – *really* OTT – gave
it a cheesy fairytale look, like the bed piled high with
mattresses in that story where the Princess can't sleep
because there's a pea underneath 'em and she can feel it
because she's so *sensitive* or because she's a *princess* or
something, which, it went without saying, was much the

same thing. Lola sighed. What was that stupid story called? 'The Princess and the Pea.' Obviously.

It had to be the biggest – and the ugliest – bed in the world. The new double bed was a fact of life, whatever Lola thought of it. But whichever way she looked at it, she found she couldn't like it any better. Why had her parents bought it? What were they, *blind*? It looked *smug*, Lola decided. Self-satisfied. A bit of a bully, with its brass-bound corners and its blustering, pompous great bedhead, and the enormous puffed-up *bulk* of it taking up half her parents' bedroom. It wouldn't bully *her*, Lola decided. No way would *she* get used to it in a hurry, big ugly thing. The Comfi-Lux had bossed its way into the house last Friday, but it still seemed like yesterday to Lola. If it thought she was going to accept it, just like that, it had better have another think coming.

Hanley's Betta Beds had delivered the giant mistake – the monstrosity Lola called it – at about half past three the previous Friday afternoon. Lola had just got home from school when the lorry pulled up and they brought it in, piece by king-size piece. Unbelievable. Bed or circus tent – what *was* it? Quilted panels like cliffs came in. Puffed-up bolsters the size of whole grannies or grandads. Polythene-wrapped Formica drawers, in all their hidden beauty.

'I can't believe I'm *seeing* this,' Lola said.

Her mother looked rueful. 'Nor can I.'

# The Comfi-Lux

More and more king-size pieces came out of the lorry Lola's heart sank when she saw them. She wanted to shut them out – *no, thanks* – but nothing would stop them nosing in at the door like the prow of a ship or the tip of an iceberg or something.

'It's *huge*.'

'It's big,' Lola's mother agreed.

In came two bulky fold-outs covered in chatty-looking satin. Those two hinged together, worse luck, to make up the king-size bed-base. In came the bedhead – horrible thing. Then the giant mattress – individually sprung, thick as a train and covered in enough polythene to gift-wrap a section of coastline.

'See that?' The Hanley's man showed them the mattress. 'Comfi-Lux – quality label, that,'

Lola stooped to read it. The label on the mattress read: '*The Comfi-Lux – your guarantee of excellence. With more than forty years of bedmaking expertise, quality, comfort and value are assured.*'

They might be assured, Lola thought, but are they worth putting up with *the worst-looking bed in the world*?

'You've got a bargain there, love,' the Hanley's man had told Lola's mother. 'Quality bed. Do you a lifetime, that one.'

But, oh, it was ugly, Lola thought. Ugly, ugly, ugly. 'Don't you think, Tom?' she asked, long after Hanley's had gone.

'Don't I think, what?' Lola's brother Tom looked in at the door.

'Don't you think it's *ugly*?'

Tom considered the Comfi-Lux. 'I think it's a *bed*,' he said.

Lola considered the Comfi-Lux from every possible angle. At least *she* wouldn't have to sleep on it, with its absurdly informative label, telling everyone how it was made, as if anyone wanted to know: '*Patent comfi pocket springing*,' the label announced. '*Each spring individually pocketed in calico for maximum comfort and support.*'

Big wows. Lola pictured each spring individually pocketed in calico. It was hard, she thought, to find a *single good thing* about the Comfi-Lux. She hated its self-important bedhead. She hated its Formica drawers and the mean little castors *underneath* it. It wasn't even comfortable. You were so high up you felt like you'd fall any minute, so quilted and stifled by it, you couldn't even feel when you'd go. OK, so it wasn't her bed – but it's ugliness somehow *polluted the house*. How had her parents *liked* it?

'You're ugly,' she'd told the Comfi-Lux, on the day of its arrival. 'You're ugly, and I *hate* you.'

The Comfi-Lux had sat primly on its nasty little castors like an overweight lady in tiny high heels. It *was* what it *was*, and that was that. Someone had actually bothered *making* it, probably in a factory, probably along with a hundred other ugly beds with lovingly nested springs. It was a *hungry* bed, Lola decided. Not what it seemed at first glance, it was posing as something grand. Posing as something grand, it had an empty space at its core. With an empty space at its core, it was a bed that would gobble you up. And in gobbling you up it would –

'Coming downstairs?' Lola's mother had shouted.

'Not yet! I'm testing the bed!'

– and in gobbling you up, *it would always want more.* It was hungry for people to sleep in it, hungry to shake off its new smell, hungry for someone to *like* it. Lola shivered. Then she slipped down off the bed. You'd crack your head if you fell off the edge. It had to be over a metre to the floor.

'What did you want such a *big* one for?' Lola had asked, downstairs.

'What's it to do with you?'

'It's *horrible*. Why did you buy it?'

'Your father bought it, actually.'

'What is he, *blind*? It's horrendous.'

'Looks comfy, though, doesn't it?' Mum said.

Tom hadn't slept well that night. Finally he'd fallen asleep fitfully, then felt like he hadn't slept at all. He woke up twitchy as a leaf on a twig, ready to drop, but never in the act of falling.

Lola looked ill over breakfast.

'I don't feel well,' she complained.

'Me neither,' Tom said. 'I couldn't sleep. I lay awake for ages.'

'That's what I did,' Lola said. 'I ended up reading a book. Now my neck really aches. I must have slept on it funny.'

'Maybe you need a new bed.' Lola's mother poured the tea. '*I* slept like a rock.'

That'd be right, Lola thought. Buy a bed like a mountain, no wonder you sleep like a rock. 'You'll have to keep your door closed,' she said, 'whenever my friends come upstairs.'

'You what?'

'I mean it,' Lola said, seriously. 'I can't have them seeing the Comfi-Lux monstrosity'

'Oh. Is the rest of the house all right, or should I redecorate for them?'

That night, Lola felt worse. All evening, everyone else had seemed unbearably irritating – were they doing it *deliberately*? – so that she thought her *head* would burst with the annoyance. By bedtime, thrilling shivers ran up and down her back. She got into bed and the night hours closed in around her. Her body ached, flushed hot, then cold, so finally she put on the light. She felt like running in to Mum, except she wasn't six any more. Finally she dozed off and dreamed of stitching fingers –

busy fingers stitching, stitching, stitching little mouths up tight. In the morning she woke up with throbbing ears and little popping lights in the corners of her vision. Her mouth was dry. She felt like she'd woken up on the edge of the world. Feeling more than slightly unreal, she crawled into bed beside her mother. The Comfi-Lux wasn't bad, she thought. It really was pretty comfi.

'You'd better stay right here today.' Lola's mother got up and felt her head. 'You've got a raging temperature. Probably this flu that's going round.'

'I've got it too,' Tom said. 'Go on – feel *my* head.'

Lola's mother felt Tom's head. Then she sent him to school. A long time after Tom had left to catch the school bus, a long time after boiled egg and soldiers and orange juice and paracetamol for breakfast, Lola heard her working. Lola's mother worked from her office downstairs. Tap, tap, tap – Lola heard the word-processor reeling out words that turned, mysteriously, into stories. Nee-breener-ner-ner – the printer churned out the pages. It would churn out pages all morning, and most of the afternoon.

Lola looked through a magazine. There was nothing much in it but fluff and some good-looking faces. She tore a few out. She lay back and thought about Hollywood and Los Angeles, and stars with tasteful-looking beds in languorous white rooms filled with plants, with turquoise pools glinting outside. She sat up and did her nails, feeling a strange reluctance to actually get out of bed whenever she needed more stuff.

In the end, she picked up a book. The bookcase in Lola's parents' room held a strange mix of romance, history, rubbish and books that went out with the Ark. They had dull-looking covers and authors with names like Laura Willcox-Harmsworth or Peter Diddley-Squashit or Mabel Dreary-Boredom. But some had magical titles like *King Solomon's Mines* or *The Seven Pillars of Wisdom*. Lola picked out *Beneath the Red Sea*, mainly because of its colour plates of bright but deadly fishes, and climbed back into bed.

She read and read and read. Soon she knew about corals, groupers, anemones and electric eels. Or she *would've*, if she could concentrate, for all the shouting outside. Nicky and Scott next door again. You wouldn't think two boys aged six and four could possibly make so much *noise*. Lola looked at the clock. It *couldn't* be three fifteen. Were Nicky and Scott next door home from school *already*?

Her lunch-tray lay crustily on the floor. Lola binned the cold cheese on toast her mother had brought her what seemed like hours ago. Then she ritualistically ate the chocolate mini-roll, nibbling off the chocolate coating first, then unrolling the sponge and scraping out the filling, then finally eating the sponge. The noise outside got worse. It sounded like balls in a skip or the start of the

Third World War. Lola screwed up her wrapper and stood on the bed. Then she opened the window and settled Nicky and Scott: 'SHUT UP, CAN'T YOU? I'M TRYING TO *READ!*'

Their jaws dropped. They looked up.

'We were only playing horses,' Nicky complained, spreading fingers grey with dirt in explanation.

'Well, play them somewhere else. I'm only ill in bed.'

Nicky stuck his neck out. 'You play 'em somewhere else. We got *racing* to do.'

Lola gritted her teeth and stuck to her guns. She got through the rest of *Beneath the Red Sea* at lightning speed, despite the sounds of Nicky and Scott jumping up and down on the corrugated iron roof of the shed adjoining the barn next door. She read all that evening, as well. She didn't even go downstairs to watch *EastEnders*.

Her mother brought lasagne up on a tray. Lola read until it had gone cold. Then she ate the corner and ditched the rest. She didn't need food on a tray. She needed to feed her *head*. That night she had a special dispensation. That's what Dad looked in and called it.

'How are you feeling?' he asked.

'Not too good,' Lola said.

'Not eating much?'

'I'm not hungry.'

'Mum says you like the Comfi-Lux. We'll sleep next door, if you like.'

'No, Dad, it's all right. Really. I'll go back to my own bed tonight.'

But her father wouldn't hear of her moving. 'You're comfy in there – it's a grand bed, isn't it?'

'It's okay, I suppose.'

'You stay right where you are. Special dispensation while you're ill.'

The next day passed, and the next. Feverishly Lola read books in bed, books she didn't even *want* to read. She couldn't stop reading so long as she lay in bed, and so long as the Comfi-Lux had her, she couldn't get out of bed. The hours slipped away in an airless dream and tasted of *Kim* or *The Treasury at Petra* or *Ring of Bright Water* or *Life and Death in the Tower of London*. The Comfi-Lux wouldn't let her go. It wanted more and more. It made Lola read beyond pleasure, comfort or sense. Finally she read in a stupor, faster and faster, and *still* she had to read more. It was making her ill. The Comfi-Lux was insatiable. She didn't care if no one believed her. Three days of insatiable reading and she was *ready* to believe that she lay helplessly under the spell of a king-size bed with a thirst for knowledge as big as its lumbar springing. What did anyone *else* care, so long as she stayed in bed and looked as though she was resting and getting better?

Except that she wasn't. She was getting worse, and Tom saw it. 'Your eyes are red,' her brother noticed, the third day she'd lain in bed. 'Been rubbing soap in 'em, have you?'

'No,' Lola said, 'I've been reading all day.' It was true. Her eyes were killing her. 'Take them away now, can't you?'

She meant her books. Tom pushed them off the bed with his foot. *Kidnapped. British Butterflies. Complete Short Stories of H. G. Wells. Great Steam Ships of the Twentieth Century.*

'Thanks,' Lola said palely. 'I can't start another one now.'

'What – you read all them in *one day*?'

'I can't stop. I *want* to get up and go to school, but the bed won't let me.'

'Yeah, right,' Tom said. Lola brushed away tears. She couldn't seem to reach Tom through the film enclosing her body. So long as she lay in bed, she couldn't seem to reach *anyone*. She felt like Katy Carr in *What Katy Did* – she'd read it only yesterday – when What Katy Did was break her back on a swing and spend her *life* in bed.

'Tom, I'm not joking,' she said. 'I want to stop, but the bed wants more. It made me read *Pictorial Knowledge* volume four today, as well as everything else. I don't think I can *take* volume five.'

Tom laughed with his mouth, but not with his eyes. He didn't know what to make of it. Something was wrong, but what? He wanted to go – to get away. He didn't want to see. 'How can it be the *bed*?'

'Sit down, then,' Lola coaxed. 'Come on. Come and sit down on the bed, if you don't believe me.'

But Tom wouldn't. 'I'm going out now, all right?' he said. 'I might be back later, OK?'

He *touched* the bed when he picked up her empty dinner tray. But he wouldn't sit down on it, she noticed.

The Comfi-Lux had been made in a hot den of spidery looms and hanging robot arms that screwed up hinges and popped little springs into pockets, Lola knew. The nightmare ran on, hotly, horribly. Each little individual spring squeaked shrilly as the robot arms popped them in pockets. 'Let us out,' they squeaked. 'Don't sew us up in the Comfi-Lux. We'll do anything,' they squeaked, 'only let us go! *Let us out! LET US OUT NOW!*'

Lola jumped up in a sweat. She ran out of bed to the toilet, then she ran back really fast. But it was too late. The Comfi-Lux sensed her presence. Of course, it knew she was awake. *Switch on the light*, the bed said. Lola switched on the light. *Pick up a book*, the bed said. Lola picked up a book. *Start reading, then*. Lola started. She read until three in the morning, red-eyed, reluctant, half dropping-off, half not. *Sit up*, said the bed, *we're not finished*.

'I am!' cried Lola. *You're not.* 'Read 'em yourself!' Lola cried. 'I can't go on! I don't *want* to read *Pictorial Knowledge*! Or *Brighton Rock*! Or *Kim*! Or the *Encyclopaedia of Rocks and Minerals*, or a *History of the Old West* – got it?'

Suddenly Lola felt as if the weight of all the world's books were standing on her shoulders. *Pictorial Knowledge*, volume five, slid heavily on to the floor. She wouldn't read any more tonight, not if the Comfi-Lux nagged her to death or smothered her slowly in a Luxurious Sleeping Experience, not if – *the bed ate her up*. Each of the individually pocketed springs inside the Comfi-Lux sighed a little as Lola lay back, exhausted.

She didn't sleep very well. By seven thirty in the morning when her mother looked in, felt her head, and went out again, Lola had thrown her arms and legs into a hundred feverish positions over most of the *not* Comfi-Lux. She tossed and turned uncomfortably – the bed seemed to be made of something unbearably knobbly, like pebbles or other people's heads – until Tom loomed in at eight o'clock.

'Oh,' she said, 'what is it?'

'You,' Tom said, 'that's what. What was all that shouting about last night?'

Lola sat up painfully. 'There was something under the mattress. I didn't sleep very well.'

'Mum says she's getting the doctor.'

'Oh?'

Tom nodded. 'Mum says, enough's enough. She's ringing the health centre now.'

'Can you look under the mattress?'

'Under the mattress? Are you kidding?'

'There's something *awful* under it.'

'There's nothing,' Tom said, 'you're mad.'

'It's the bed,' Lola wailed. 'It's punishing me.'

'It's *punishing* you? What for?'

'I didn't read enough last night – we only did volume five last night, when we ought to have finished volume six.'

'We?' Tom asked. 'Who's *we*?'

'I. Me. The Comfi-Lux.'

Tom smiled. He tried to make it look natural. 'Well. Got to go. See what the doctor says.'

'See what the doctor says about what?'

'You,' Tom said, 'you know you're *seriously* –'

'What's that over there on the floor?' Lola flapped her arm impatiently. 'Over there, by the door – can't you *see*?'

Tom picked it up. A hard, dry grey-green pea. 'It's – a pea,' he said.

'I knew it.' Lola fell back in the bed.

'It's only a pea,' Tom said. 'It must've come out of something.'

'Bring it here,' Lola ordered.

Tom brought it.

'I *told* you there was something under the mattress.' Lola examined the pea. 'No *wonder* I couldn't sleep.'

'Why would there be a pea under the mattress?'

Tom asked. Why *would* there?

'To test me, of course. I told you.'

'To test you. Right. Of course.'

Tom backed out. He looked at Lola, deep in the monster-sized bed. Her small head looked lost against its pompous-looking headboard. The Comfi-Lux seemed to enclose her. Soon it would gobble her up completely. He'd come home from school and there'd be nothing left of Lola except a pile of books, a half-drunk drink of Lucozade and a – pea. And that would be all. *And the Comfi-Lux would have won.* Tom shuddered. It was only a bed – an ugly bed. A bed with a big personality. And not a nice one, at that.

Lola had closed her eyes. She hadn't even noticed he'd gone.

Tom cleared his throat. 'Yes. Well. I'm going now'

'Uh-huh.' Was that a goodbye?

'Smell you later,' Tom added.

'Not-if-I-smell-you-first.'

The voice was deep, almost pompous. It didn't, Tom thought, even *sound* like Lola any more.

'Can you tell those kids to shut up?'

'What – Nicky and Scott next door?'

'They're getting on my nerves, all right? Plus I need a drink.'

'Get me this. Get me that. Get it yourself,' Tom said. 'What are you, the Queen or something?'

'I have to ask you, don't I? If I can't do things myself.'

Lola had lain for a week in the Comfi-Lux now. The changes were obvious to everyone. Her voice was low and weak, her tone imperious and demanding, her eyes dull, her skin-tone duller, her parents increasingly anxious. Words like *glandular fever* were being bandied about. Until Doctor Inman called, that is. Doctor Inman brought a new word with him. The word he brought was *malingerer*. Lola hadn't heard it, so she didn't really know. She hadn't even asked what Doctor Inman said. She didn't know a malingerer was someone who pretended to be ill when they weren't ill any longer. She didn't know Dr Inman had prescribed fresh air, activity and school on Monday. She wasn't even curious. She didn't care what he – or anybody – said.

'Look at this,' Tom said.

'What?'

'It's about eccentric people.'

'What is?'

'This article in *TV Quick*. Brian Wilson, musician, stayed in bed *three years*, it says here. Became enormously fat.'

'Why did he do that?'

'I don't know, he just did. That's what'll happen to

you, if you don't watch out. There's more. Eccentric millionaire Howard Hughes –'

'I don't care, I'll do what I like!'

'And everyone else gets to *let* you? Run the world from your *bed*, why don't you?'

'Well, I'm doing okay.'

'No,' Tom said, 'you're not – you're doing rubbish. You're making everyone wait on you hand and foot. But not me – as from now.'

'Shut the door on your way out,' Lola ordered weakly.

'I might,' Tom said, 'or you might have to shut it for me.'

Lola struggled upright. 'SHUT THE DOOR!' she yelled.

'You're scary you know that?' Tom said.

But it wasn't really Lola, Tom thought, the miserable Hitler in bed. She wasn't like she normally was, so long as she was in it. How could he get her *out* of it? Would she really get up on Monday, like Doctor Inman said? It wasn't really Lola who was scary. *The really scary thing was that bed.*

'Getting up day,' Tom announced in Lola's ear on Monday. 'Come on, shift it. Let's go.'

'Leave me alone, I said,' Lola buried her face in the clean white deeps of the Comfi-Lux. Tom stripped the duvet back. How small she looked. How frail. Like a small white sail on the ocean.

'Mum says get up or get hungry.'

'What?'

'You heard,' Tom said. 'There's nothing wrong with you.'

'That's not what Mum said.'

'It's what Dr Inman told her.'

'It isn't.'

'It *is*. Shall I get her?' Tom took a deep breath. 'Mum – Mum! Come here!'

Lola's mother pounded upstairs.

'What is it? Has something happened?'

'She won't get up,' Tom said.

'I really don't feel like it, Mum.' Lola's voice fell an octave or two. 'I don't really think I'm up to it, do you? I mean, I wouldn't want to collapse in school. I wouldn't want them to think you'd sent me in when I wasn't well. They might not think it appropriate.'

'Appropriate?' Lola's mother stared. 'I don't know why you're talking like this, Lola. Dr Inman said you can go back to school any time you're ready.'

'But I'm *not* ready, do you see?'

Lola's mother looked at Tom. Tom swallowed. 'I think,' he said, 'she ought to get out of bed.'

'I agree. You've had a fever. You're feeling weak. How can you tell how you feel if you never get up?'

'I *do* get up. I acquire knowledge. I have individually pocketed springs.'

'Lola! This isn't funny!' Lola's mother felt frightened, she didn't know why. 'I want you up and about today. Mr Snell sent you some homework. You can work on the kitchen table, then tomorrow you go back to school.'

'Tomorrow,' Lola echoed.

'You can keep that silly voice for telling jokes. One more day,' her mother warned.

'One more day,' Lola echoed.

'I mean it.'

'You mean it. I understand.'

'Just so long as you do.'

Lola seemed strangely unlike herself. Her mother withdrew with the feeling that what she had said hadn't sunk in at all.

The day passed as other days had. Lola knew it was serious. She didn't even read. Instead, she lay in a light dream and thought about headboards and rivets, factory-finishing and superior springing of the type she knew she had. She thought her mother came in – and nagged her and flung down some of her clothes. Lunch downstairs, her mother had said, *when* you're prepared to come down. But lunchtime came and went, and Lola didn't go down. Nicky and Scott came home from school and took up howling outside. Lola listened. It didn't seem fair. They had such *life* outside.

The front door slammed downstairs and her brother Tom came home from school and *still* Lola hadn't got up. Tom pounded straight upstairs. She could see the displeasure in his face. 'I thought you were getting *up* today.'

'Tom – please –'

'I told 'em you're throwing a sicky at school. You've got *loads* of stuff to catch up.'

'You don't understand, I can't just –'

'What's *happening* to you?' Tom demanded. 'You're turning into this huge great bloater who knows everything in the world and never goes out. What's the point of *that*?'

'The biggest,' Lola said faintly, 'and the best – that's what it's about.'

'Biggest and best – like the bed, you mean? You're turning *into* that bed.'

'That's so stupid – you're sick.'

'Why don't you ever get *out* of it, then?'

'I'm going to school tomorrow, Mum said.'

'Good job,' Tom finished. 'That bed's got it over on you. You need to get legs and a *brain*.'

Tom shut the door and went out.

'Tom please – wait!' Lola called him back. Nicky and Scott's shouts had dwindled away next door. This was, very possibly, the end. 'Tom! Please! Help me!'

'What did you say?' Tom put his head round the door.

Lola struggled to repeat it. But her voice had sunk

pompously low. 'I need an adjustment – HELP – twelve hundred pocket springs – ME – give truly luxurious support –'

'Yeah, right,' Tom slammed out, disgusted.

'TOM!' Please come back, Lola thought. 'TOM!' *Please*. 'TOM!'

'*What*?' Tom's head reappeared at last.

'Tom – please – my very last chance –'

Lola put a foot out of bed. It took all her strength to do it. She reached out to Tom with both arms. 'Tom,' she said, 'please help me.'

Tom was at her side in a moment. 'I want to,' he said. 'How?'

'Pull – pull me out of bed a bit, first.'

Tom pulled. 'What else?' he said, urgently. 'Tell me.'

'Nicky and Scott,' Lola whispered. Her voice was her own, at least. 'Please, Tom. *Get Nicky and Scott.*'

'They're noisy. Why would you want them?'

'Just get them. Please,' Lola whispered.

'What on *earth* – ?'

Lola's mother opened her bedroom door and took in the scene open-mouthed. Nicky and Scott from next door. Bouncing around on the brand-new Comfi-Lux bed! And Tom! And Lola! Making so much noise they couldn't *hear*.

'Yay!' Nicky screamed. 'I got to *bomb* 'em! I bomb-bomb-bomb –'

'I bomb you *back*!' Scott boffed his brother with pillows, again and again. 'An' I *get* you I do –'

'An' I get you –'

'*Oh, no! Mars attack!*' Nicky pointed at Tom, bouncing hugely behind Lola, already armed with a pillow. 'Red alert! Bounce 'em off! Bounce 'em – go on – *bounce* 'em –'

Nicky and Scott upped their bouncing, and for a moment it was touch and go who would bounce *who* off the bed. Tom and Lola weighed in with their pillows, but Nicky and Scott had a good rhythm going already. Nicky bounced mightily, peaking just as he spotted Lola's mother open-mouthed at the door.

'Nicky and Scott! Tom and Lola! Can you get down off the bed?'

The Comfi-Lux sighed with relief. Its headboard banged against the wall as Lola bounded off it. Lola's mother looked at her. Her cheeks were flushed, her eyes bright. She looked, well, so much *better*. Like the little girl she'd once been. Little and bright and shining.

'I don't know *what* you all think you're doing.' Lola's mother tried to look stern.

Nicky and Scott climbed down. Tom put the pillows back.

'Please, Mum,' Lola said, 'we're only playing

Mars Attack.'

'Not on the Comfi-Lux, you're not. Lola, I'm surprised.'

'So'm I,' Lola admitted. 'But it's broken the spell, don't you see?'

'Spell? What spell?'

Lola's mother looked from Nicky and Scott, to Tom and Lola – flushed, panting, giving out rude health like anything. *What a change*, she thought. *How like herself Lola looks. How well. How full of life.* Suddenly Lola's mother realized just how pale and how ill – how *bed-ridden* – her daughter had been. Looking at her now – eyes shining, playing with Nicky and Scott as though she were six years old – it was difficult to remember the world-weary invalid of yesterday or this morning. Even the sick-room *air* had lifted. And Tom – Tom, especially, looked pleased and flushed, as though he'd done something clever. They *all* looked pleased and flushed – all except the Comfi-Lux, which looked rumpled and out of sorts. It had lost its dignity all right. *Perhaps it had needed to.*

'*What* spell?' Lola's mother repeated, knowing, in the moment she said it, exactly what spell it was.

'Oh, *you* know,' Lola said. 'I wasn't so good, was I? But now I'm bouncing, I'm better, *if* you know what I mean.'

'Now you're bouncing you're better.'

Tom cleared his throat. 'She's right,' he said. 'Don't you think she looks great?'

'She *does* look great,' Lola's mother admitted.

'I feel great,' Lola said.

'And we did bouncing, all right,' Nicky said, twisting his fingers.

'An' it's a *horrible* bed an' we *biffed* it,' his brother Scott added.

'Thanks very much,' Lola's mother said. 'Let's hope you haven't biffed it too much.'

'It's just – the Comfi-Lux needed sorting,' Lola explained in a rush, 'and we've sort of *broken it in*, you know? And now it's like any *other* bed, only bigger and better, of course, and I knew they could do it – Nicky and Scott, I mean – and I had to ask Tom to get them and then we bounced the newness away, and all that – and it was getting above itself you see, and it wouldn't let me get up – and now I feel *brilliant* – don't I, Tom? – and I think I'll get up and run a bath.'

The Comfi-Lux sat squarely on its dented little legs while Lola ran on and on. It was a broken bed. There was no obvious damage. Its newness – its *uniqueness* – gone, it was just a rather ugly king-size bed. Its twelve hundred individually pocketed springs still nested cosily inside its sumptuously layered mattress. Its headboard wasn't really damaged. Comfort, Quality and Value were still Assured. But the spell was truly broken. It would never be the same bed again.

'And tomorrow I've got PE so I need my sports shirt

clean, plus my geography file needs sorting for Mr Reeve and I'll have to ring Josephine Naylor to find out what maths we're doing.'

Bursting with health and energy, so full of life she was practically walking up walls, she'd probably stay up all evening, and practically half the night. Tom and his mother watched Lola gabble on. She had so much to say, it seemed she would never stop.

# Bigglesmith

'Shel, *don't*, I mean it.'

Shel and Nina Gibbons lay helplessly on the floor. Or Nina Gibbons did, anyway. Her sister Michelle was getting on top of her this time. Literally. Every time she play-fought Shel, Shel had the upper hand. Strong as a wire monkey, Shel was tough and agile and *nothing* could throw her off.

'I'm not in the mood, Shel, don't –'

Usually Shel would sit on Nina and pin down her arms with her knees and do disgusting things like gob on her face or blow raspberries or roar in her ears. Then there was tickling, and bird's nest. Bird's nest reduced Nina Gibbons to helplessness even just *thinking* about it. Her limbs turned to water. Her strength leaked away in pleading laughter. She became completely helpless and unable to resist Shel at all. And did Shel ever know it.

'No! Not bird's nest! Please!'

Shel produced a finger in mid-air. 'Here's a birdie wants a nest –'

'Don't, Shel, I *mean* it!'

'– a nest in a nice, warm place –'

Nina felt her limbs turn to water. 'Don't,' she begged, 'Shel, don't.'

'– and it's coming in to find it –' Shel wiggled her finger and brought it inexorably closer '– and any minute now, it'll –'

'Stop – I don't want it – *no*!'

Nina made a huge effort to throw her sister off. But Michelle was bigger and stronger. Her sister's wiggling finger zeroed inexorably in.

'– here it comes –'

'SHEL, GET OFF ME!'

'– here comes the birdie to nest in your –'

Nina twisted hysterically.

'– NECK!'

The finger wiggled, paused – then darted in and 'nested' under Nina's chin, where she absolutely couldn't *bear* it, in the most ticklish niche of her neck.

'*Shel, don't, please don't, please, Shel –*' Nina Gibbons wasn't in the mood for fighting today, she really wasn't. Sometimes fighting was fun. More often it started out fun and then got an edge of annoyance. The trouble was, as usual, the mood was on a knife edge. The feeling of not being able to stop the tickling, whatever she did, made her helpless before the tickling started. Also it made her annoyed. Why couldn't Shel see? Now and again, she didn't mind. But when she *did* mind – like today she minded – why couldn't Shel understand?

'Stop it, Shel, I'm not joking!' Nina fought her sister off, weakly, desperately, knowing she couldn't win. 'Get *off* me, will you? I'm not in the mood!'

No matter how much she begged or struggled or ordered her off, Shel would always sit on her *just that bit* too long. That was Shel's trouble. She didn't know when to stop. Nina twisted and wriggled, getting really angry, this time. 'Get off me, Shel. *I really mean it this time!*'

'Ah,' Shel said, 'she means it.' And tickled her sister some more.

Nina Gibbons shrieked, 'Get off, I'll wet myself!'

'You better not.'

'I *will*.'

'Shame she can't get up.'

'Get off me, *right now, Michelle Gibbons!*'

Nina Gibbons went mad. Erupting from all directions at once, she bit and kicked and heaved and struggled, this time in deadly earnest. The struggle got vicious; stalemated for a moment or two with both sisters straining for a hold over each other's legs, then Nina lost it completely, flailing her arms and legs like she meant to shake them off.

'Can't you tell when I've had enough. – I mean it, *get off me now*!'

Two or three really vicious bangs on the back, and Michelle Gibbons got off her sister at last. And not a moment too soon. 'Hey,' she said, in an injured tone, 'hey, that really hurt.'

'I told you MILLIONS of times to get off,' Nina flamed, in capital letters, really upset this time. 'You always go on too long. NEVER do that to me again.'

'No need to hit me like *that*.'

'When I say get off I MEAN IT I *hate* the way you don't stop.'

'So half-bang my *back* in, why don't you? How was I to know?'

'You never listen, whatever I say. Can't you *hear* I mean it?'

'Not really. I thought you were laughing.'

'Oh, yeah. I *sound* like I'm laughing.'

Shel shrugged. 'I thought you liked us mucking about.'

'I would, if you knew when to stop.'

'Oh, and you do?'

'I do, as it happens, which is more than *you'll* ever know.'

'Calm down.'

'I *am* calm, thank you.'

Nina Gibbons wiped her face with her sleeve. Her rage had spent itself. But she'd felt like half *killing* her sister. Where was the sense in *that*?

'OK,' she began. 'We're going to fix this once and for all.'

'Oh, yeah?' Michelle examined her back in the bedroom mirror. 'See those red marks where you bashed me?'

'Yes, well, I didn't mean to. What we need to do,' Nina Gibbons said carefully, 'what we need to do, is think of a *word*.'

'What word?'

'A word you only use when you really *mean* it. A word you can say to stop fighting – or whatever – and when you *use* that word, that's *it*.'

Michelle pulled down her sweater again.

'Mmm,' she said, 'that's not bad.'

'This word, you don't use it too often, right? But when you do, the other person has to stop *right away*, no matter what they're doing. And this word means you're *desperate*, so no more bird's nest.'

'OK,' Michelle said, 'I get it. So what's the word?'

'The word is . . .' Nina Gibbons thought furiously. Something memorable, something funny, something you could screech out with the full weight of fury behind it, something odd, something final, something . . . 'The word is –'

'Malaga!'

'What?'

'Malaga!'

'I heard you. Why?'

'I don't know' Shel shrugged. 'Denise Sumner's going to Malaga on holiday this year.'

'Oh,' Nina said, 'good reason.'

'How about Brad, or Paul?'

'What – you're actually going to stop tickling me if I yell Brad or Paul?'

'I might.' Shel considered. 'Then again I might not.'

'It has to be something – big. Something we don't forget.'

'Humungeous?' Shel suggested. 'Supercalifragilistic-expi—'

'No, I don't think so.'

'Plinth?'

'Warthog?'

'The indices on the hypotenuse?'

'Snappy one, that.'

'British summertime?'

'Jellyfish?'

'Intestines?'

'*Intestines?*'

'Irritable Bowel Syndrome?'

'Excuse me?'

'Callisthenics?'

'I'm not lying on the floor yelling Callisthenics! What *are* callisthenics?'

'I don't know,' Nina admitted. 'How about custard pudding?'

'Crusty Semolina!'

'Big Fat Eskimo Toenails!'

'Rubbery Wellies!'

'Bigglesmith!'

'What?'

'You heard me, *BIGGLESMITH*!' Nina yelled it this time.

'Bigglesmith.' Meaty, beaty, big and bouncy, it was a word you wouldn't forget in a hurry. It was a big word with a big – and quite silly – ring to it. A ring you couldn't ignore. Shel rolled the word round her mouth. A slow smile spread to her eyes and made her face quite pleasant.

'Bigglesmith. That's *it*.'

ᘘ

'Bones of Contention,' introduced Freeman Leland, 'will be a Complementary Studies extension featuring *debate*. Anything from capital punishment to genetic engineering. Your lesson, your time, *your* debate.'

'What about hunt protestors?' Colin Denton demanded.

'What about them?'

'Do we hang them or clone them?'

'Colin, that's for you to debate, and for me to regret you want to.'

Freeman Leland smiled. The faint American twang in his voice made him sound cool and reasonable, no matter what he said.

'It isn't funny, Colin. How would *you* like to be hunted?' Nina Gibbons put in.

'Um, I think I'd like it.' Denton grinned, and his face sank into his neck and his neck sank into his chest and the rest of him quivered in the smug, self-satisfied way that made Nina Gibbons want to hit him.

Nina felt her flesh crawl. As well as having a dimpled bum-chin and being physically repulsive, Denton shot small animals with air rifles at weekends. She knew, without having to think about it, that whatever side she was on in any school debate, Colin Denton would be on the other. No matter what it was about. 'You're just weird,' she said.

'I'm calling this series of debates *Bones* for now,' went on Freeman Leland, 'and I hope we can worry some interesting bones of contention between us and really hone our debating skills in this Complementary Studies extension. It's going to be whatever you make of it. And if you think of a better title you'd better let me know.'

That'd be right, Nina thought. Freeman Leland Rules – If That's OK With You. Easily the coolest teacher in school, Freeman Leland liked to think he had a way of putting things which made students feel they'd *contributed*. That was his whole approach. It didn't always work, especially with insects like Denton. But that didn't put him out. Freeman Leland was keen on student input. Keen on debate of all kinds. Keen on *talking things through*. Nina and Shel had spent serious time imagining him over breakfast. *Can you pass the butter, if you feel you can make that commitment? Would I like some porridge? That's for me to decide and for you to let me. Toast? It's a value judgement – can I get back to you on that one?*

'We can talk about anything, right?' David Rainer asked.

'Anything voted interesting enough to discuss.'

'So we *can't* talk about anything.'

'It's up to you to put it across. *You* sell it to *us* for discussion.'

'What's the point?'

'The point?'

David Rainer frowned. David Rainer was dark and intense and no one messed him about. 'Nothing's going to change things. What's the point in talking?'

'Things like?'

'I don't know. Stuff we do in geography. Over-population in Pradha province. Creeping deforestation. What's the point in *debating* it? Nothing's going to fix it.'

'There's no debate, if we all agree,' Freeman Leland agreed. 'We're not going to save the world. What we want is a bone of contention.'

'Something no one agrees with?'

'Something it's possible to disagree with. You throw us a bone, we'll gnaw it,' Freeman Leland invited. 'Anyone else here think talking about things is pointless?'

'It is if you have ANTS,' Nina Gibbons bowled him.

'ANTS?'

'Automatic Negative Thoughts.'

'Right,' David said sarcastically, 'lots of people have those.'

''Specially hunt protestors.' Colin Denton rippled, his chin disappearing into his neck fat.

'I'm delighted you're getting behind this, Ten GB,' Freeman Leland congratulated the class. 'Plenty of input from everyone makes for a lively discussion. If you'd like a topic discussed, would you run it by me before Friday? You don't have to, of course. You can simply propose it in class. It's your debate, after all.'

'How about journalism?' Nina Gibbons said. 'Journalists get a lot of stick, but *I* think they do a good job. Plus they stand in battle zones –'

'This is Nina Gibbons for *News at Ten*,' Denton put on a newscaster's voice. 'Reports are coming in that I'm changing my name, because most of my fan mail's from monkeys –'

'Something else stupid from Denton.' Nina made a face. 'Why doesn't that surprise me?'

David Rainer thought ethics in journalism might make a pretty good topic, but no one ever knew why because Richard Fargo fell off his chair and brought Martin Rickard down with him. Noise levels rose pretty quickly after that. Freeman Leland raised his voice, 'In the event that no one tables a motion –'

'I tabled Rickard, sir,' Richard Fargo volunteered. 'We're playing bar-billiards, right, and I tripped him up with my cue and decked him on the table –'

'In-the-event-that-no-one-tables-a-motion –'

'Sir, what kind of motion?' Richard Fargo widened his eyes. Someone made a straining noise. 'Would that be a *regular* motion?'

By the time he'd explained that *tabling a motion* meant proposing a topic for discussion in a certain formalized way so that everyone else could disagree with it, Freeman Leland had completely lost control of the class. Nina watched him scornfully. Freeman Leland was weak. He meant well, but his big puffy words were weak. Words widdled out of his mouth. They didn't mean anything at all.

'Could I have your attention, Ten GB? If no one tables a topic for next week's Bones – Richard Fargo and Martin Rickard, I assume you're getting up to present a topic for discussion?'

# Bigglesmith

'I was, but now I'm not.' Richard Fargo sat down again. Martin Rickard sat down on top of him.

'One student per chair please, Martin.'

Freeman Leland waited until Martin Rickard had seated himself noisily behind Richard Fargo. Then he cleared his throat. 'Unless anyone has a serious contribution, next week's Bones will take the form of an open debate on what we'd all like to talk about. Thank you for your attention. And that winds it up for today – except –'

'Except what, Mr Leland?' Denton asked. 'Except I don't have to do it?'

'– except, of course, for the *issues*. Things that concern you and me, things that concern just about everyone. Think about those issues and how you might get them across. Words,' finished Freeman Leland, 'meanings. Thoughts. Conclusions. Between now and next week, okay, let's *think* about what we say.'

Let's *think* about what we say. Nina Gibbons shouldered her bag and walked home with David Rainer through the Grange Road Mall. The Grange Road Mall was her shortest way home, but it didn't always appeal. Today it appealed less than usual. The warm air, filled with shop smells and faintly tinged with fast food, made her feel slightly ill. She hurried on, feeling different today, somehow special, and found herself reading the signs.

*Ginger's for Hair – New Look Styles a Speciality.*
*Flowers Express – Same Day Blooms Say So Much.*
*NAILED for Nail Extensions & Facial Makeover*
*TANNERS – Medically Approved Sunbed Treatment*
*for Safe & Easy Tanning.*
*KingBurger Easy-Over Breakfast Only Two Ninety-Nine!*

The trouble was, no good shops. The Grange Road Mall had been going downhill for years. It had been glossy once. Once it had been the place to go. Now only sad people shopped there. But, still, they shopped a lot.

*Crimpers for Hair and Beauty.*
*Top Look!*
*NEW SEASON SALE!*
*Shoe-be-dos, TRAINERS HALF PRICE.*
*SuperFare at Grange Rd Mall – Individual Provençal Pies*
*£1.75 All This Week.*

The signs were bad. The signs, Nina thought, of the way she'd been brought up to live. How would it look to an Eskimo? Someone from an Eastern bloc country where most of the shelves stood empty? A baby from Pradha Province? There was so much on offer. Too much. Why hadn't she noticed the smell of *too much* before? She always walked home through the Grange Road Mall. She didn't always stop. But today she stopped.

Today she stopped and lingered . . .

'Come on,' David said, 'what's the matter?'

. . . and it seemed to Nina Gibbons that she was seeing the Grange Road Mall for the very first time in her life. The cheesy-looking glass lift – like Charlie's Great Glass Elevator – whispered up and down between the artificial palms. Above it, the balcony clattered with afternoon shoppers having a quick and crowded cuppa in the Buttery. Everywhere, people shopped.

'Nothing's the matter,' she said. 'I was thinking about Bones of Contention.'

The Sock Stop and the Shirt Shack and the Loose Box racing-themed Snack Spot. Shopping – *wanting things* – never stopped. Like tickling, it ran on and on.

'What are you doing for next week's Bones?' David asked.

'Something Colin Denton *isn't*. I *hate* Colin Denton,' Nina told him.

'This is Nina Gibbons for *News at Ten*. Here on the battlefront, exchanges have been brisk –'

'BIGGLESMITH!' Michelle screamed.

'– with Nina Gibbons coming under continuous fire and little in the way of –'

'*BIGGLESMITH!*' Michelle screamed again.

'– relief, the light at the end of the tunnel seems a –'

Nina Gibbons sat on top of her sister and wound up her outside broadcast.

'– long way away. Get *up*, then,' Nina told Shel, getting up herself. 'What are you waiting for, Christmas?'

Where had she got her strength from tonight? It must be anger with Denton. Or maybe with her parents, rowing again as usual. It was one of those evenings for fighting. Anger was in the air. You could practically *see* it, Nina thought.

'I *said* Bigglesmith.' Michelle got up crossly. 'I thought you were meant to *respect* it. What's the point, if you don't?'

'I got up, didn't I?'

'Not right away, you didn't,'

'I'm sorry *what* did you say?' Nina flicked Shel with a towel.

'*Bigglesmith!*' Shel put the bed between herself and the towel. 'Pack it in, it hurts!'

'Abuse of Bigglesmith, in any case,' Nina accused her. 'You're devaluing Bigglesmith by its overuse in inappropriate contexts.'

'Excuse me?'

'The thing about Bigglesmith is, it's an unbreakable swear-on-your-honour –'

'Can you stop flicking me *now*?'

Nina stopped and sat down. It was getting on her nerves. The row downstairs had been going on since teatime.

Something to do with money – it usually was. Soon Mum and Dad would calm down. It would all blow over, as usual. Why did it have to start?

'Are you all right? Nina?'

'What do *you* think? I *like* hearing them rowing downstairs?'

'It'll be all right. They don't mean it.'

'Why do they *do* it, then?'

'What's the matter with *you*?' Shel said.'You're really aggro tonight.'

'It's Denton,' Nina lied. It *was* partly Denton, though. 'I really, really hate him. Plus, we're doing debates at school.'

'And?'

'Denton made a prat of himself again today. No one can debate *anything* with Denton around. He doesn't know *how* to debate.'

'So?'

'So I'm trying to think of a topic. But I *know* he'll shout me down.'

'Don't let him.'

'How do I stop him?'

'What's the debate about?'

'Anything. Whatever. We've got to think of things.'

A door slammed somewhere downstairs. Angry voices rose and fell. It was worse, Nina thought, when they stopped.

'They're getting worse,' Shel said.

'The sound of firing seems unceasing, here in these battle-scarred hills –'

'Nina. It isn't funny.'

'No,' Nina said, 'it isn't.' Parents' rows were never funny. 'I never said it was.'

'Hear that crash? They're throwing things.'

'Correction. One of them is.'

'Think Mum's all right?'

'Mum's all right,' Nina said. 'Sounds a lot worse than it is.'

'Should we go down?'

'Too scary.'

'You better be right,' Shel said.

A door opened. A door closed. Then the front door slammed.

'Dad going out, I expect,' Shel said.

'About time.' Nina got up. Her stomach felt filled with angry words. Words she felt like shouting. 'I'm going out – want to come?'

Shel considered. 'What – now?'

'I have to get out, OK?'

Shel shrugged on a jacket. 'OK. All right. I'll come.'

The Grange Road Mall showed its dark side by night, the dank and evil-smelling passages where sad people slumped and slept and sometimes didn't get up. Its everyday face had been bunkered by steel blinds and shutters and PREMISES PROTECTED BY ALLSTAR SECURITY SYSTEMS signs. Apart from American Fry and V.J. Video, a pub or two on the corner and the London Late-Nite Shopper, everything was closed. The tellies in Gleason's Electrics' window showed highlights of the day's events on *Newsnight Extra*, ten newscasters smiling blandly from ten TV sets with ten different prices – but there wasn't a lot else to see.

Nina pressed her forehead to the window of Gleason's Electrics and allowed herself to feel angry. The news moved on to Bosnia, then Albania. All that arguing, Nina thought. At home and away – wars and disputations, everywhere, all over the place, all the time. If only they stopped to *listen* and *think*. If only they could all *hear*. The Day in Parliament flickered up on all ten tellies at once. 'Order!' the Speaker bleated. 'Order! Gentlemen, please! Order! Order! Order!' But still no order prevailed.

'Got enough for some chips?' Shel asked. 'I've got eighty-three p.'

They rounded the corner on the chip shop. Opposite the chippie, outside a pub called the Three Jacks, something was going on. Something pretty scary. Something involving David Rainer.

'What is it?' Nina stared. 'Looks like David.'

Three figures – three Jacks, maybe – had David Rainer on the floor. Nina could hear the blows land. It wasn't a friendly bundle. They were really kicking him in.

'Nina, come back!' Shel screamed. 'Nina! Come – back – here!'

Through the legs of the psychos kicking him in, Nina glimpsed his face across the dirty, fag-littered floor. David Rainer's eyes appealed to Nina Gibbons across the length of the Grange Road Mall. She had time to notice *the exact pattern* of the floor tiles before she started running.

'*STOP!*' she shouted, running. '*DON'T YOU DARE! YOU JUST LEAVE HIM ALONE!*'

David Rainer lay curled on the ground. For long and horrible moments, whenever they wanted, wherever they could, the three jacks stood and kicked him. Then the moment ended. The three jacks looked up.

'GET OFF HIM!' Nina Gibbons shouted. 'DON'T YOU KNOW WHEN TO STOP? *GET OFF HIM AND LEAVE HIM ALONE!*'

Time seemed to pass really *slowly*.

'*Nina, come back!*' Michelle screamed. David Rainer looked curled-up and small. The back of his neck looked red. Nina Gibbons shouted and shouted and shouted, without thinking, without knowing, without stopping. She didn't know what she shouted. She'd never made so much noise.

'BIGGLESMITH!' she shouted.

*Whaat?*

'BIGGLESMITH! BIGGLESMITH! BIGGLE-SMITH!'

# Bigglesmith

The three jacks were running away.

*Shut that noisy cow up! Leave it! Come on! Now!*

Nina watched them go, screaming she didn't know what, so long as it was LOUD and David Rainer's eyes were closed and they didn't look at her that way any more, the way they'd looked at her a moment ago, across the chip-littered, dirty floor. She shouted through fear and anger. Then she shouted through blood. She hadn't known she'd bitten her cheek until she'd opened her mouth and yelled.

And in the Grange Road Mall, with its fountains, she'd shouted, '*BIGGLESMITH*!'

⬛

'Got a topic, have we?' Denton asked, unpleasantly.

'That's for me to know and for you to find out.'

Nina made her Denton face, a particularly acid smile. It usually shut him up. She checked her notes for *Bones*. She'd tabled the motion. Run it by Freeman Leland. What else could she do, but look a lot better than she felt? Starting a killer debate, with her arguments thought out beforehand, was the least she could do for Denton. And even that was kind. *Don't let him shout you down*, Shel had said. *Say what you think and stick to it.*

'Wait for it, Denton,' she told him.

Freeman Leland cleared his throat. 'So far in Bones of Contention, I'm pleased to say we've covered a lot of ground. Topics so far have included bloodsports,' he looked at Colin Denton, 'homelessness, the death penalty, should zoos be abolished and, last week, violence on television. The motion before the house this week has been tabled by Nina Gibbons –'

'And seconded by monkeys.' Denton grinned.

'You'll have your chance in a moment, Colin.' Freeman Leland frowned. 'The motion before this House today is that "Shop till you drop is an immoral idea. When is enough enough, in view of Third World want?" Have we a seconder?'

Everyone looked at Nina. Nina felt waves of panic. She might have put it better. She saw now, they wouldn't understand. But someone understood. David Rainer held her with his hunted-looking eyes.

'I'll second that, sir,' he said. 'I can't put up my hand.'

'Winded by running in from maths, Mr Rainer?' Freeman Leland joked.

David Rainer winced. He wore Elastoplast from brow to cheekbone. It made him almost good-looking. 'Something like that, sir,' he said.

'. . . and as a confirmed shopper, I'd just like to say *enough shopping*.' Nina Gibbons wound up her argument for ethical shopping. She felt she'd put it well. Better, at least, than the motion she'd tabled earlier. 'When we're kids our mums and dads tell us when enough is enough.

Now we can buy almost anything we want, we have to learn to say it for ourselves.'

'Why?' asked Colin Denton.

'Ethical shopping means only buying things you *need*, made by people who get paid a decent rate. Else we're robbing someone, somewhere.'

'Why?' asked Colin Denton.

'Don't you ever feel there's too much choice?' Nina floundered a little under the Denton stare. 'Like, you go into the supermarket and there's just *too much* of everything and it's obscene that we need it all?'

'No,' said Colin Denton.

'Me neither,' said Richard Fargo.

'And there's stuff like mange-tout peas and people in Zambia are paid, like, one *p* to pick them, and the supermarkets charge a *pound*.'

'So,' Denton said, 'what's that to you?'

'Like you never go shopping or something,' Martin Rickard put in.

'I *do*, that's the point.'

'You think you're so big with your *ethics*,' Denton sneered.

'No,' Nina said, 'I don't.'

'Why don't you take your monge-the-toot whatsits and –'

'I just think we could all have less, not more, and no one would even mind.'

'– why don't you go and –'

'Enough. That's all I'm saying.'

'– get *stuffed*.'

'Arooo! Ar-ar-arooo!' Richard Fargo threw back his head and howled like a wolf for no other reason than that he felt like it. 'Ar-ar-aroo!'

Nina felt tears welling up. Couldn't *anyone* see what she meant?

'Let's get back to basics,' Freeman Leland reasoned. 'Is it or isn't it reasonable in a consumer society, to want to –'

'She loves herself,' Denton said.

'Shut it,' said David Rainer.

'She loves herself to death –'

'Nina fancies gibbons,' Richard Fargo added. '– and they love *her* –'

'Shut *up*!' David shouted.

'– that's why she's got hairy arms –'

'– arms? did you see her *legs*?'

'I told you, shut it *now*!'

'Nina Gibbons –'

'Tells some big ones –'

'*Leave her alone, why don't you?*'

'She's got fleas –'

'On her knees –'

'BIGGLESMITH!' David shouted. '*Don't you know when to stop?*'

# Bigglesmith

'So,' said Freeman Leland, over a hot chocolate, 'what does it *mean*, exactly? Enough's enough? Stop doing whatever it is you're doing? Sit up and *listen* to me, will you?'

'All of those things.' Nina nodded. 'Plus, it means this is *it*.'

'It, what?'

'It – *I mean what I'm saying*. Like in the Second World War, when Hitler invaded Poland, we should've said Bigglesmith!'

Denton, Rainer, Richard and Fargo nodded sagely and agreed. Fargo had bolted his milkshake already. Already busy angling for another, he wasn't too busy to nick Martin Rickard's chips. He would eat what he could while it lasted. It wasn't *every* day Complementary Studies went to town. Not every day they finished a debate with Coke 'n' chips at Kingburger, courtesy of Freeman Leland. But this would be the last time. The motion is carried, Freeman Leland had said. This House believes that *enough is enough*. This brings our series of debates to an end. Shall we celebrate?

That would be the end of debates, Fargo wasn't sure why. What had it all been about? Nina Gibbons had got pretty mad. Rainer went ape at Denton. Then he'd shouted that word. That word had changed things, somehow. What did that word *mean*?

'It's a big word,' Leland said. 'It takes a lot of courage.'

'There's other big words,' Nina said.

'Bigglesmith's special,' said Denton.

'Look inside,' David said. 'That's what Bigglesmith means.'

'And listen up,' Denton added. 'It means listen up, as well.'

'It saved me last night,' David said.

'Where was it, again?' Fargo asked.

'Over there, under the sign.' David pointed through the window at the Three Jacks pub sign opposite. 'Right outside the Three Jacks. That's where it saved me,' he said.

Everyone considered the spot reverently. David had told them all about it. How three kids had kicked him in when he'd gone out to get some milk at the Late-Nite Shopper. How he'd thought he was in for it, until Nina Gibbons showed up. How she'd run towards him – when she could have run away – and shouted and shouted and shouted: 'BIGGLESMITH GET OFF HIM! BIGGLESMITH STOP NOW! BIGGLESMITH! BIGGLESMITH! BIGGLESMITH!'

How it had freaked out the kids who jumped him when they didn't understand what it meant. How they'd nicked off without a thing. How *Bigglesmith!* had saved him. How it kind of came out when he needed it. How he couldn't forget it, ever, now he'd got it inside his head.

'What were they like?' Denton asked.

'Three kids. I don't know.' David Rainer shrugged. 'They didn't get anything.'

'Good for Bigglesmith.' Freeman Leland smiled. 'It's quite a concept, Nina.'

'I know it's silly, really.' Nina grinned. 'I don't know what it means.'

But everyone else did, it seemed. *Bigglesmith!* had reached them all. Even Colin Denton.

'I think it just means stop what you're doing and *think*,' Martin Rickard put in.

'That as well,' Denton said.

Freeman Leland nodded. 'It seems to mean *integrity* also.'

'I know what's right,' David Rainer offered, 'and I'll stick by what I say.'

'Exactly,' agreed Freeman Leland. 'Character. Trust. Honesty. Meaning what you say.'

'Right,' Denton nodded, 'that's the one. It means all that, as well.'

'It kind of means *enough*, too,' Nina added thoughtfully. Everything she'd tried to say seemed to boil down to this word. 'Enough-and-be-thankful, kind of.'

'*Bigglesmith!* means all of it.' David Rainer agreed.

'It's a kind of feeling there's no words for.' Richard Fargo surprised himself. 'That's what *I* think, anyway.'

'Plus it means time to *think*,' Martin Rickard insisted.

Integrity. Honesty. Stop and Enough. It meant something different to everyone. *Bigglesmith*! had grown big and meaningful, Nina thought, with the power everyone had given it who *wanted* a truthful word which made what people thought *count*. More power to its elbow, if it could. In a world full of words no one listened to, there was nothing a spear of justice like *Bigglesmith*! couldn't do. Think of the things it *might've* done. Old Anne Boleyn might've yelled it and kept her head. Elizabeth the First might've yelled it and stopped the Armada. If their daughters popped up and yelled it, it might even stop parents rowing. At least, it might make them laugh.

*Bigglesmith!* would *make* people listen. And once they'd stopped and listened, they would have to stop and think. How about *Bigglesmith!* on the world's nuclear waste transporters? It could become a watchword. A quiet word. A people's word. It was a people's word already. It belonged to everyone who could say it and *feel* what it meant.

'The world needs a word like Bigglesmith!' Freeman Leland said, thoughtfully.

'That's just what I was thinking,' Nina Gibbons nodded. 'And, you know? I think –'

'Yes?'

'I think maybe, just maybe, if I get to be a journalist, I might be going to tell them.'

'That's just what they want,' David said. 'Outspoken people like you.'

'It's what they're going to *get*.'

'You have a *dooty*.' David smiled. 'Get out there and spread the Word.'

'She's started already,' Denton said.

'In the beginning, was the Word. And the Word was –'

'*Bigglesmith*!'

Nina smiled. 'You got it.'

# NICK

It started with *Attack of the Fifty-foot Woman*. That was the film his mother was watching when Charlie Williams first spotted the Spirit of Nicotine. Nick, he called him, for short, when he'd seen him once or twice around the house. Nick rode around on his – Charlie Williams' – mother's shoulder. She carried him around with her always. She didn't know he was there, of course. But Charlie knew he was there.

Nick was spiky, pale yellow, very thin and long-drawn-out, with spiteful red eyes and a head the shape of a starfruit. He looked a lot like Jack Frost, except he was yellow. Charlie saw Jack Frost, too, but he didn't often admit it, even to himself. Jack Frost was the Spirit of Winter, of course, but Charlie didn't know that, until he met Nick as well. Then he began to understand. Everything had a spirit. *It was just that some people could see them.*

There were nice ones and nasty ones, of course. Charlie was clear about that. Nick was one spirit his mother could do without. He rode around on her neck most days and made her want to smoke more, and the more she smoked, the more spiteful he grew, the firmer and more spiky he appeared. He was pretty full of himself, the night Charlie Williams first spotted him when his mother was watching a film. The night he first saw Nick, Charlie Williams said: '*Wha-aa-tt?*'

His mother turned to look at him. Behind the smoke spiralling up from the ashtray on the arm of the settee, the Fifty-foot Woman strode through cities and brushed off tanks like gnats. 'What is it, Charlie?' his mother said. 'Charlie, are you all right?'

'Um, I don't know – what's *that?*'

'What's what?'

'Something – on your shoulder –' Charlie's mother brushed her shoulder irritably. Charlie saw, with fascination, her hand pass *right through* Nick.

'Isn't it time you were in bed?'

'I am, I'm just –'

'What are you staring at?'

'*You.*'

'Have I grown a third eye, or something?'

She might as well have, Charlie thought. Instead, she'd grown a monster on her back. He'd come down to kiss his mother goodnight, when he saw, on her shoulder, a *thing*. The thing was the Spirit of Smoking. And it lived on his mother's back. Charlie watched, fascinated, as Nick curled his pale yellow tail around her neck. The pale yellow spikes running down his back rippled as she moved. He looked actually quite *heavy*, if spirits could ever weigh much. Charlie's mother didn't realize, but her shoulders were actually *bent*.

'A third eye?' Charlie said. 'No, I – you look strange.'

'I know, it's this make-up. I knew it was too dark when I bought it.' Charlie's mother lit a fresh cigarette. The Spirit of Nicotine winked. 'I knew I should have gone for Summer Shandy.'

'Summer Shandy?'

'Foundation. I haven't used much yet. I might take it back tomorrow. What are you waiting for? Come and kiss me goodnight.'

The Fifty-foot Woman crushed a few towns while Charlie struggled with himself. It took all Charlie's courage to kiss his mother goodnight, with the red-eyed Spirit of Nicotine in his face. Charlie could smell him now. He smelt rank and bitter and greedy – greedy for power over his, Charlie's, mother and over anyone else he could sit on. He would never sit on Charlie. Charlie was wise to him, now.

"Night, then,' he said to his mother.

"Night, love,' she said, exhaling smoke.

Charlie went upstairs in a state of fear and confusion. *What other spirits were there?* He looked around his bedroom and the Spirit of Bedrooms was silent. He cleaned his teeth in the bathroom, and the Spirit of Toothpaste winked at him in the mirror. It looked a lot like him, with toothpaste round his mouth. He went back into his bedroom, and the Spirit of Cactus had written him a letter. He picked it up and read it: 'MORE WATER WHAT AM I DEAD?'

Charlie watered his cactus. He felt sorry now, that he'd neglected it. He felt sorry its rusty brown spirit had had to climb out of it to complain. Charlie filled a glass of water and set it beside his cactus. He wouldn't forget it again. Not now he'd seen its *spirit*.

He went to sleep in a whirl of clashing ideas. What would the Spirit of Water be like? The Spirit of Tea? Or Coffee? What about the Spirit of Garlic? The Spirit of Gas Central Heating? Charlie thought about it, and he *knew* the Spirit of Petrol looked like a geek in glasses. It wore a jacket that shivered in rainbow colours, like petrol in a filling-station puddle, and it looked a bit seedy sometimes.

Charlie's mind raced. Would the Spirit of Chocolate be hot and exotic with Aztec feathers in its hair, or would it be cool and knowing? What would the Spirit of Alcohol look like? Or the Spirit of Cinema Popcorn? How about the Spirit of Bowling? Would the Spirit of Railway Stations have dust and crisp packets over it, or pigeons in its hair? What about Football? Would the Spirit of Tarmouth United be bulging with useful muscles, or would it look sickly and nerdish, since they'd just lost three games in a row? How about the Spirit of Pizza? Or the Spirit of Builders' Merchants? Pasties? Kippers? The Video Hire? *The Spirit of Fish and Chips*?

At last Charlie Williams felt the Spirit of Sleep and Dreams softly alight on his shoulders. In no time at all, he'd let it carry him away . . .

In the garden next morning, the Spirit of Runner Beans surprised him on top of the fence. It was long and red and it pulsed with lights. Charlie saw it was *energy*. He'd never talked with a spirit before. He didn't know quite what to say.

'Hi,' he said, 'Runner Beans. I didn't know you could – I didn't, I mean – oh, this is *silly*.'

The spirit helped him out. It didn't talk at all. It simply sent him *growing* thoughts and glowed with manic energy. It filled him up completely, until he thought he'd grow or go mad. The runner-bean plants were growing, he saw, even as he watched them. Their tips swayed and felt for a hold on the fence, on sticks, on each other. Their brilliant scarlet flowers felt for bees. *Pollinate. Grow. Make beans.* This was all their spirit said.

It was hard to think of anything else, so long as you watched them.

At last Charlie tore himself away, but he still felt like growing over breakfast. He sighed and stretched his toes.

'What's up with you this morning?' Charlie's mother stacked the dishwasher.

'I feel like – oh, I don't know'

Charlie's mother looked at him. 'You're restless,' she said, 'like last night.'

'I know that,' Charlie acknowledged. 'It's just, I'm fed up with things.'

'What things?'

'I don't know. Things as they *are*.'

His father had gone out already, or he might have been able to tell him. Charlie got on well with his dad. He got on well with his mum, as well, but in a different way. Charlie's mother looked smart today. She worked behind the perfume counter in a glossy department store. Sometimes she brought perfumes home. Charlie knew all the names – Utopia, Excess, Renewal, Mantra, Psyche, Karisma! Today she smelled of Utopia. Charlie's mother sold a lot of Utopia. It was one of her most popular fragrances and a top niff in Charlie's book any day. Charlie thought he'd rush upstairs and smell the bottle and see what its spirit looked like. Probably she looked like a dream in silk, and her voice would be just like chocolate. The spirit of Utopia had to be a *babe*, if she looked the way Utopia smelt. Charlie was about to get up when his brother Warwick came in, smelling quite strongly of catfood.

'Stupid cat.' Warwick turned on the tap. 'Stupid cat's bowl tipped up, and I got it all over me – yuk.'

Warwick washed catfood off his hands. The Spirit of Catfood tried following him into the kitchen and got caught in the door behind him. It sicked up and spat and then melted away like a stain. Good job, Charlie thought. The Spirit of Catfood was a nightmare. He'd never seen anything like it. *A cat made of meat with forks and bones and dead things stuck all over it* – the Spirit of Catfood had to be the ugliest he'd seen.

Warwick towelled his hands disgustedly. He'd been feeding the cat in the garage, because Charlie never fed it, so *he* had to – something *else* he had to do that Charlie didn't. Warwick was younger than Charlie by two years, five months and twenty-one days, which made Charlie the boss of Warwick by a not inconsiderable margin. Another thing which made him the boss of Warwick was that Charlie could remember all the stupid things he'd done, like the time Warwick had got lost in Denham's department store, when he'd gone in with Mum when he was little, when she'd only just started her job.

'Remember the time you got lost in Denham's with Mum?' Charlie said, enjoying the Spirit of Warwick, which looked like Warwick, aged four.

'No,' Warwick said. 'Remind me, why don't you? I've only heard it half a million times.'

'Remember you hid in the luggage department? And then you followed Mum? But *it* wasn't Mum at all, *it* was –'

'Some other woman, ha, ha.' Warwick picked up his schoolbag. 'I'm going now. Coming, or what?'

Or what, Charlie thought, was his preferred option today. Who wanted to go to school, with the world so *spirited* and flavourful? No way, he'd like to have said. I've got things to *see*.

'Come on, then,' Warwick said, crossly. 'We better go some time this *century*.'

It was no use. He'd have to go to school now, Charlie could see. It wouldn't matter what he said. What wonderful things he could see. *Please, sir. I saw the Spirit of Runner Beans and the Spirit of Catfood this morning. Can I have the day off to see the Spirit of Everything Else?* He couldn't see it going down too well. So he couldn't go into town today; that didn't stop him wanting to. Charlie burned to see the Spirit of Shopping Malls, the Spirit of Sportswear, Surf-shops, Piers, Pavilions, Arcade Games, Bus Stations, Fountains, Country Fried Chicken, HMV Records, Smith's, Boots – the Spirit of *Everything*. A whole world waited out there. But it would have to wait a bit longer. Today he would have to settle for the Spirit of German Grammar, probably some seventy-year-old milkmaid who got very cross when you spoke. Or maybe the Spirit of Maths, a jumble of sharp, mixed-up numbers. Or Art, which looked like Van Gogh.

''Bye, Mum,' Charlie said. 'We're going now.' Then he said, 'Mum, I know it's hard, but – I *wish* you'd give up smoking.'

Charlie's mother looked at him. Nick glared down at him redly from her neck. He raised his spines a little. He showed his yellow teeth. Better not upset him, Charlie thought. He doesn't want me to say that, Charlie thought. Who knows what he might do?

'Did you take some dinner money, Charlie?' Charlie's mother stood by the door and applied her final lipstick.

'Mum, did you hear what I said?'

'I wish, too,' she said, sadly. 'Have a good day now, won't you?'

Charlie kissed his mother goodbye and smelled Nick's nicotine breath. Nick's grip on his mother had tightened, Charlie knew. It would grow tighter still at work with every coffee-break. He hated to leave his mother with Nick round her neck all day. Why couldn't Nick get off her back? Why couldn't he, Charlie, save her? The Spirit of Nicotine read this thoughts. It crackled threateningly when it moved. But only Charlie could hear it. Better not upset him, Charlie thought.

He couldn't dislodge Nick, Charlie knew. Not without some help.

'That's the spirit,' Charlie's dad said. 'Well done, Charlie boy.'

His mother had gone out of the room leaving her smoking ashtray for a moment. Charlie had stubbed out her cigarette and hidden it under the table. He wouldn't be too popular when she got back. But Dad was behind him, at least.

'Mum won't like it,' Charlie said. 'She's told me off already.'

'Get over it, Charlie,' she'd told him. 'I know what you're trying to do, but it's just annoying, all right?'

'Never you mind, Charlie boy,' Dad said. 'Let's hope she gets the message.'

Charlie had been sending his mother plenty of messages lately. He had, in fact, launched his Stub It campaign a week ago last Tuesday. Something had to be done. Nick had got fat and complacent. He lay around Charlie's mother's neck with his pale yellow tail hanging down. It looked grotesque. She didn't know — how could she? On Saturdays Nick ballooned overnight, when Charlie's parents met friends at the pub and stayed to talk for hours. Sundays, he took it easy. His body grew heavier, yellower. His death-breath stank of furnaces and ashtrays, of frightful bitter acids and acrid things that ate away your stomach. He'd taken to winking at Charlie over meals and trying to inch his tail over Charlie's neck, so that Charlie found himself wondering what cigarettes actually *tasted* like. He'd almost caught himself tasting one. It had happened one night last week.

One night the previous week – Monday night, it was – Charlie had been doing his homework in the middle of the kitchen table, when he'd felt a touch on his neck. He looked up. Nothing but the Spirit of Homework, he thought morosely. But the miserable-looking Spirit of Homework had pulled up a pew and lost itself in its knitting. In its place stood the Spirit of Nicotine, crackling ever-so-slightly.

'Get away from me,' Charlie said. 'You stink.'

'Don't be like that,' Nick wheedled. 'You owe me, am I wrong?'

'I *owe* you? I don't *think* so.'

'I let you see everything.'

'You did? You mean,' Charlie lowered his voice, 'the *spirits* of everything?'

'That's right,' said the Spirit of Nicotine. 'And the least you can do is try me.'

His mother's packet of cigarettes lay on the kitchen table.

Charlie balked. 'As if.'

'Go on,' Nick wheedled, 'taste one.'

'So you can sit on my neck?'

'I could sit on your neck anyway.'

'No,' Charlie said, 'you couldn't.'

Nick's eyes glowed. 'I could *try*.'

Charlie got up and opened a can of beans.

'What other spirits are there?' he said. 'I want to know them *all*.'

'Oh, there's lots,' Nick said, putting his feet up. 'As many as you like.'

'How come I never saw them before?'

'Have you ever *looked*?'

Baked beans in a bowl with fingers of bread was a favourite with Charlie for supper. He got out a pan and heated his beans and thought about ways to trap Nick. It wasn't going to be easy to outwit him. How *did* you get rid of an unwelcome spirit? A spirit as *well in* as Nick?

'Did you try giving him a taste of his own medicine?' the Spirit of Baked Beans enquired.

Charlie dropped his spoon in the pan. '*What* did you say?' he said.

'Him. Old Nick.' The Spirit of Baked Beans fished out Charlie's spoon and licked its fingers. It looked like a big fat baby dressed in orange. 'He's a nasty piece of work, he is. Did you try giving him a taste of a spirit *he doesn't like*?'

'Excuse me?' Nick said to it, smartly. '*Should* you be sitting on a work surface next to a cooker?'

'Don't try that with *me*.' The Spirit of Baked Beans flicked hot beans at Nick. 'I know what *your* game is.'

Charlie whipped the pan away and poured beans into his bowl. The Spirit of Baked Beans chatted until he'd eaten them. Then it had had to go. Something to do with a meeting. In some transport café.

'So who don't you like?' Charlie said.

'Hoo,' Nick said, 'hoo, hoo.'

'Between you and me,' Charlie said.

'Between you and me, I'd like a smoke.'

Suddenly Charlie saw. His only power over Nick lay in *what Nick wanted him to do.*

'So would I,' Charlie said. Charlie took out a cigarette and put it into his mouth.

'Go on,' Nick wheedled, 'light up.'

Charlie flicked the lighter. A little flame jumped up. Spirits of Smoke and Fire fizzed and whispered in his ears.

'Try me,' Nick wheedled. 'Where's the big deal?'

'I may,' Charlie said. 'I just might. But which *is* your least favourite spirit?'

The lighter flame danced in Nick's eye. He hissed and made a circle on the table. His pale yellow triangular spines quivered with the desire for Charlie to light up. Round and round he circled. Suddenly, back he came in Charlie's face. 'I don't care for that smell in the garage.'

'What smell?'

'That *mess* called the Spirit of Catfood.' Nick shuddered. 'It has no style. It's savage.'

'I'm not crazy about it, either.'

'Fine tobacco and *catfood* – ugh. The very thought. It's revolting.'

Charlie brought the lighter close, then closer. Then he laid it down. 'I don't think I will, after all.'

'*You don't know what you're missing!*' Nick hissed, circling angrily on the table.

'Oh,' Charlie said, 'I think I do.'

That had been more than a week ago. Since then, the Stub It campaign had taken considerable risks. Nick was dangerous, Charlie knew. But stubbing out her cigarettes was making his mother cross. It was helping Nick win her over. Thoroughly at home by now on Charlie's mother's back, Nick cleaned his claws in Charlie's face. He clicked and coiled his tail. He winked and blinked his eyes. He made Charlie's mother frantic if she thought the shops had closed. No matter how much Utopia she sprayed on at work, Charlie's mum always smelled of Nick. He made her short of breath on stairs. Get up, whenever he wanted. And the larger Nick grew, the more bent and worried she looked.

Charlie's mother had to do whatever Nick wanted, and there was nothing Charlie could do about it. Nick lay and blinked at him nightly. *Ea-sy – ea-sy – ea-sy.*

He was fighting a losing battle. Warwick knew it. Charlie's dad knew it. Dibley the *cat* knew it. The worst of it was, so did Charlie. Charlie exchanged a look with his dad as his mother re-entered the room. Wait for it, Charlie thought.

'Charlie, where's that cigarette?' she demanded.

'It went out,' Charlie said.

'No, it didn't. You stubbed it out. You'll have to get off this, Charlie.'

Nick grinned wolfishly over Charlie's mother's shoulder. Charlie felt depressed. He wasn't supernatural, was he? How could he fight a sprite? How could he hope to win? He found his mother's jumper over the chair, the jumper she wore round her shoulders to watch TV – the monkey jumper, they called it, because it was woolly and brown and huge and made of matted mohair. He might as well sit in the monkey jumper as try to explain how he *felt*. He pulled it on and sat in it, but *even the monkey jumper smelled of Nick*. Its spirit looked just like a monkey. It sat on Charlie and grinned. Charlie pushed it off. This was getting stupid. What next? The Spirit of Teatowels?

Warwick came in with a very full glass of orange juice and set it down gingerly on the table. The cat slipped in behind him and began to wash itself. Warwick smelled vaguely of catfood. The Spirit of Catfood tried following him in round the door, but as usual it had trouble with the sticks and forks and fish-heads and lids of catfood tins that stuck out all over it, like lumps in a Christmas pudding. *A cat made of meat with dead things stuck in it.*

# NICK

It looked like a badly made bird's nest, with a big, jowly cat in the middle, except that it smelt a lot worse. It had eyes like a fish, fishbones for whiskers and a loose, mealy mouth with forgotten bits of meat hanging out of it. Wherever it went, it carried its own cloud of flies. Poo – *yuck*, Charlie thought. He watched in fascination as the Spirit of Catfood nudged its way in round the door. Little did Warwick know he had a friend.

Why couldn't Charlie get smelly sometimes? Taking the tops off catfood. Right after breakfast and dinner. It made him want to *hurl*. Warwick kicked the door shut, annoyed. 'Stupid cat's always leaving the door open.'

'Possibly you are,' Dad said.

The Spirit of Catfood belched and let out a gas.

'Pooh!' Warwick held his nose. 'Put Dibsy out, someone, will you?'

Warwick meant Dibley the cat. Warwick had named the cat Dibley for a joke, but no one ever called it by its name. Mostly they called it Catface or Smell or Junkfood, because that was what it ate. Charlie picked up the cat and put it out in the garden. He watched it wander off into the runner beans. The Spirits of Evening are *abroad*, he found himself thinking. Then he went back inside.

'What's that on your shoulder?' he suddenly asked Warwick.

Warwick looked up. 'What?'

'That – spiky thing. Keep still.'

It was nothing at all. Charlie tried, but he couldn't pick it up. It had looked like a spike – a triangular, pale yellow spike – which had melted away as he touched it and left a suspicious smell.

'You been smoking?' Charlie asked.

Warwick snorted. '*Would* I?'

Maybe, Charlie thought. If Nick got a foot on your shoulder. That's *it*, Charlie thought, that really is. That's just about the *end*.

That night, he got up at midnight. He got dressed and went into town. The glorious Spirits of Evening were abroad in carefree bands, swaggering in the side-streets and spilling out of clubs. They danced in the lights of the bandstand and all along the sea-front. The sea lapped Charlie's feet as he walked along the sand. It didn't care if it lapped his feet, or if it didn't. It didn't care about anything, and its spirit was too big and boundless to be seen or understood, at least by the likes of himself. Charlie turned back towards town.

The town led him on and on and Charlie followed. He walked the greasy late-night streets and a sad young man in a sleeping bag asked him for money. Charlie gave him all he had, but the young man hardly noticed. Charlie walked in the park and the Spirits of Roses and Japonica soothed him as he passed. He passed the aviaries in the Pleasure Gardens, and the hot-eyed Spirits of Parrots followed him as he went.

# NICK

Charlie danced in fountains. He ran through glittering arcades. He window-shopped for his wish-list, and the Spirits of Reebok and Nike came to join him. Charlie ran on, through streets filled with girls in short dresses who linked arms and shouted at taxis and giggled and fell off their shoes. Charlie could see their high spirits. They looked like fizzy fireworks or popping neon balloons. They were pretty funny to watch. A few girls, Charlie noticed, had mini-Nicks on their shoulders. He hoped they wouldn't get weighed down. They looked so bright and bubbly.

Charlie ran on and on. The Spirits of Fishes depressed him, hunting and sucking the walls in the dark aquarium, but the Spirit of Kingburger filled him up and sent him on his way. Low spirits, high spirits, cut-price spirits, impossible spirits – Charlie Williams saw them all. Best of all – he saw it in the shop windows as it flitted from pane to pane – he thought he saw *the Spirit of Charlie Williams*.

When Charlie Williams got home his world was teeming. More and more spirits of more and more things thronged his mind and clamoured for his attention. They filled the garden. They filled the house. He could hardly get in at the door.

This is stupid, Charlie thought. He'd thought he'd have a snack but he couldn't even sit *down*. The Spirit of Breakfast Cereal, the Spirit of Butter and Sugar, of Bowls and Plates and Spoons – they sat in the chairs, they were in the fridge, the cupboards, they were even in the *oven*, he could see them through the door. Charlie got in a panic. He held his head. He went upstairs. The Spirit of Teeth, the Spirit of Maths, the Spirit of his Pencilcase, the Spirit of his own Jumper –

'STOP!' Charlie cried. '*ENOUGH!*'

'Enough?' said Nick. 'But Charlie, we've only just started.'

'What do you mean?' Charlie said. 'You can get off my bed *right now*.'

'Oh,' Nick said, 'I don't think so.' And he crossed his legs with a scraping sound. 'Unless, of course, you really have seen enough?'

'That's what I said, didn't I?' Charlie was pretty upset. 'I want you to go away. And take all these other ones *with* you.'

'Well, now,' Nick said smoothly, 'I can't do what you say, unless, of course, you –'

'Try me? No *way*!' Charlie said. 'I'll never get rid of you, *unless* –'

Charlie raced downstairs to the darkened garage. He flipped on the light. *There* – stacks of Dibsy's catfood, in little tins with ringpulls. Plaice and Cod. Beef with Heart. Duck with Turkey. Turkey with Chicken. Chicken with Game. Game with Rabbit. Rabbit with Liver and Gravy. Which would be the smelliest? he wondered. Probably

Plaice and Cod. You couldn't beat fish for smells. And smells were what he wanted. Quickly pulling a ringpull, he forked Plaice and Cod Chunks with Extra Vitamins for Strong Teeth and a Glossy Coat into Dibsy's smelliest bowl. He paused and listened. Now what? 'Come on, then,' he said. He turned off the light. '*Come on, then. I know you're there.*'

Charlie waited. The Spirit of Catfood sneezed and got up heavily. It wheezed a bit as it walked, and bits of meat *fell* off it and melted away. Charlie darted up the stairs. He waved his bowl. *Come on.*

Up in Charlie's bedroom, Nick lit a fresh cigarette. The smoke curled up in spirals and settled over Charlie Williams's things. His mother would think he'd been smoking, even though he hadn't, even though he *would*, before too long. Soon he would get the taste for it. It was only a matter of time.

'No sense in hiding, Charlie.' Nick tapped ash on the floor. 'Charlie, is that you?'

The door swung back. Instead of Charlie Williams, the nightmare Spirit of Catfood stood in the door. It sneezed a few times. It didn't like smoke. It didn't like smoke at *all.*

'Now, Charlie,' Nick said, 'let's talk about this –'
The Spirit of Catfood growled.
'After all,' Nick said, 'your mother can't do without me.'
The Spirit of Catfood hissed and raised its hackles.

'Charlie,' Nick said, 'I thought we were *friends*.' And he drew in his pale yellow tail.

'What gave you that idea?'

Charlie threw his smelly fork. The Spirit of Catfood sprang. Sticks and flies and rotting meat flew off it in all directions. Nick yowled and howled and stretched himself out into thin yellow smoke and wafted away down the stairwell. The Spirit of Catfood gave chase, well up the garden and down the road, and down the *next* road after that. Charlie Williams listened. Yowling. And howling. Fading away. Then nothing. Then peace and quiet.

It would come back when it had finished, Charlie supposed. He pictured the Spirit of Catfood surprising the postman. Or maybe it wouldn't. Charlie looked around his quiet room. He looked in vain for the Spirit of Maths or Teeth, or the Spirit of Prickly Cactus. In vain for the Spirit of Everything. The spirits, that night, were still.

Hi, this is Charlie. I'm actually forty-two, now. I wrote this story, about the time we had Nick in the house, because I see Nick now and then on someone's shoulder, and I really think they should know what old Red-eye's *like*. These are old memories now. This is actually a story about my brother, know why? I don't mean Warwick – well, I'll tell you.

# NICK

Around the time I set the Spirit of Catfood on Nick and it drove him away – I'm remembering now, from a long time ago, but it seemed just about the same time – my mother got sick every morning. 'I don't feel like smoking or eating,' she said. 'I feel really sick in the mornings.'

She never smoked ever again. And seven or eight months after that, my new baby brother was born. I begged them not to. But they did it anyway. My new baby brother – that's right – they called him *Nick*.